From
Beaton's
to Beach
Haven

A CAT GHOST

BH G

A Publication of the New Jersey Maritime Museum

[I]

ISBN:

Softcover: 978-1-948346-25-2
Hardcover: 978-1-948346-26-9
EBook: 978-1-948346-27-6

Library of Congress Control Number: 2017964070

Dedicated to

David Beaton and Sons

To the men who built A Cat Ghost, kept her in repair
throughout the summer and provided her with repose during
the long winter months for over twenty years.

CONTENTS

Preface VII

I. Background
  1. The A Cat from 1922 to 1992 1
       Appendix 1: E.L. Crabbe's Account 6
       Appendix 2: Mower's Letter 9
  2. Why Ghost? 9

II. Building Ghost
  1. The Woodshop 13
  2. Two Sweisguth Plans: the Hull 17
  3. Framing, Planking, and Decking 24
       1. Preliminaries 24
       2. The Core Structure of Ghost 25
       3. Framing and Planking the Hull 32
       4. Preparing for the Deck 46
       5. The Deck in Place 52
  4. The Last Rivet 54
  5. Coaming, Cabin and Xynole 59
       1. Cabin Sides and Bending Jig 59
       2. Coaming 63
       3. Covering the Deck 65
       4. The Cabin Completed 66
  6. Centerboard, Rudder and Tiller 72
       1. The Centerboard 72
       2. The Rudder 74
       3. The Tiller 79
  7. Cabin Doors 81

III. Oil, Paint and Varnish
  1. Preparation and Application 83
  2. Traditional Colors 87

IV. Spars and Sail
  1. Two Sweisguth Plans: the Sail 89
  2. Mast and Boom 93
  3. Sails 96

[V]

V.   **The Launching**
   1. Out of the Shed for Viewing.. 101
   2. The Ceremony: Speech, Verse, and Song.............................. 106
   3. The Christening 112

VI. **Seven Times Bay Champion**
   1. 1994 Disaster followed by Recovery 117
      Appendix: The BBYRA Race Course 134
   2. 1995–1998 Ghost Wins but is Challenged 135
   3. 1999–2000 New Hands on the Tiller 142

VII. **Down Bay to Little Egg**
   1. An Outstanding Race Course 149
   2. The Rheingold Mug.. 151

VIII. **The Crew**
   1. Various Tasks Distributed among the Crew 161
      Appendix: Out of Control 169
   2. A Special Appreciation 170

IX. **A New Home**
   The New Jersey Maritime Museum 175

Index of Subjects 181

PREFACE

In recent years there have been several new books and articles that focus on the A Cat, a twenty-eight foot, Marconi rigged catboat, which is peculiar to Barnegat Bay, New Jersey. Like its predecessors, this book too focuses on the A Cat, but it differs in picking out a particular A Cat called Ghost, which was built in Brick, New Jersey at a venerable boatyard: namely, David Beaton and Sons. Indeed, the book is in part a celebration of Beaton's role in reviving and maintaining the A Cat Class. In particular, the longest chapter in the book is devoted to the building of Ghost in the main shed at Beaton's boatyard. The framing of Ghost, the planking and decking are recorded in detail as are the construction of Ghost's cabin, its cockpit and spars. The various stages are illustrated by a unique collection of photographs, which along with the expository text, makes clear the meticulous care with which the craftsmen at Beaton's worked.

The idea for writing this book came from Bill Fortenbaugh, for whom Ghost was built and who was able to observe the building process as it developed. In addition, much of the English prose is his—choice of word and sentence structure—but it would be a mistake to put Bill forward as the author of the book. There are many other contributors whose time and concern made it possible to undertake and to complete the book. To begin at the beginning, there is Dick "RT" Speck, who photographed the building of Ghost, the launching and much else. It is no exaggeration to say that without his photos there would be no chapter on building Ghost and that the chapter on launching Ghost would be a dry piece of prose.

No less important are the contributions of the workers at Beaton's boatyard. There is Tom Beaton, whose interest in the A Cat Class is well known. Without his approval Ghost would never have been built, and without his willingness to review and to describe Dick Speck's photos, the exposition of the building process would be spare and faulty. Much the same is true of Paul Smith. Important to the building process, he devoted abundant time to reading manuscript, not only offering verbal suggestions but also taking time to write corrections in the margins of the manuscript as it developed over many months. In addition, there is Russ Manheimer, who worked on Ghost before returning to a business career. He contributed to the section on cabin doors and to that on the Last Rivet. Finally there is Mark Beaton, Tom's cousin, who not only made sails for Ghost but also is responsible in large measure for what is said in the book concerning the design and making of sails for A Cats.

Contributions by persons who crewed on Ghost are numerous. That is hardly surprising, since Ghost raced over 22 years and sailed with a crew of seven or eight. From the original crew, Ed Vienckowski and his wife Bev, who set up the book for publication, must be mentioned. So too John Dickson and Rod Edwards. who would have wanted to contribute but deceased before writing began. Also to be counted among the original crew is the big man Rich Miller, who came aboard for the second race of the first season. Among crew members who came on later, mention should be made of Jim Cadranell, who replaced Rod, and Ellyn Shannon, who joined the foredeck crew. In addition, there are Dave Hoder, Greg Matzat and Mark Kotzas, who might be referred to as members of the youngest generation. Finally, special mention should be made of Dan Crabbe, who joined the crew in the seventh year, often skippered Ghost and contributed significantly to the present book by supplying documents and making clear who was who, when A Cats were new on the Bay.

There are also the officers and supporters of the New Jersey Maritime Museum, Jim Vogel and Deb Whitcraft, John and Gretchen Coyle, who together made the transfer of Ghost to Beach Haven possible. Their contributions are largely to the final chapter on Ghost's new home.

Not a few other names have made their way into the text, sometimes accompanied by photos that give life to the names. It is no longer possible to recall the names of everyone who provided individual photos—the existing collection runs over 22 years—but two persons may be mentioned here as representative. One is Laureen Vellante, a professional photographer, who contributed striking photos of Ghost drifting in light air. The other is Loraine Gough, a gifted amateur, who has an eye for special moments on the race course.

Finally a few words concerning arrangement, format and style: Although the book is arranged in continuous chapters, I-IX, there is a difference between the first chapter, the next three, and the final five. Chapter I is concerned with background, both the earliest period when A Cats were first built (1922-1925) and what preceded and prompted the building of Ghost (1992). Chapters II-IV focus on the work done at Beaton's boatyard: in particular, the construction of Ghost's hull and spars as well as the oils and paints that would be applied to the several parts. These three chapters have a didactic character that goes beyond the particular moment. For persons new to building wooden sailboats, they provide a detailed introduction to the parts that make up an A Cat and how the parts are put together. Chapters V-IX are less didactic. To be sure, there are reflections on how to sail an A Cat and win races, but the tone is lighter, and the focus is on a particular boat and the particular people, who were responsible for Ghost's successes and failures.

Nodding to elevated style, abbreviation is kept in check. E.g., instead of "Pt. Pleasant", "Point" is spelled out. On the other hand, in giving references and introducing examples standard abbreviations are preferred: "e.g." means "for example", "ibid." is used for "in the same place", and "fig." covers photos, drawings and sketches.

The following publications are cited by title in the text of this book:

A Cats, a century of tradition, by Gary Jobson and Roy Wilkins, White River Junction VT: Nomad Press 2005.

"American Catboats" by Edwin J. Schoettle, in *Sailing Craft* 87–108.

"Beaton's *Ghost* Keeps Alive the A Class of Catboats" in the program of the *Old Time Barnegat Bay Decoy and Gunning Show*, 1993, p. 18-20.

"Catting Around Barnegat Bay" by Craig Ligibel in *Sailing* magazine Nov.-Dec. 2016.

Sailing Craft, a collection of chapters edited by Edwin J. Schoettle with Drawings by H. Parker, New York, NY: Macmillan 1928.

"Toms River Cup, The" by Edward Crabbe in Schoettle, *Sailing Craft* p.366-374.

Published for the first time are:

"Class A Cats" by Edward Luis Crabbe, March 25, 198(?)2.

"Letter" by Charles D. Mower to Edward Crabbe, Jan. 5, 1923.

I
BACKGROUND

1. The A Cat from 1922 to 1992

Thanks to several recent and not so recent books and articles, it is well known that the first A Cat, Mary Ann by name, was designed in 1922 by the naval architect Charles Mower of New York City. The boat was built for Charles McKeehan, a federal judge in Philadelphia. The builder was Morton Johnson, whose yard was situated on the border between Point Pleasant and Bay Head, New Jersey. Mary Ann was an immediate success. In her first season, 1922, she won the Barnegat Bay Yacht Racing Association (BBYRA) summer series for Catboats. That success will have encouraged others to follow McKeehan by commissioning the design and construction of new boats.

Indeed, there was a veritable boom in building A Cats. In 1923 four new boats were built: Edward Crabbe had Bat built by Morton Johnson according to a Mower design, and Frank Thacher had Helen built at Hopper's Basin also according to a Mower design. The other two boats built in 1923 were designed by Francis Sweisguth. One was Tamwock, which was built by John Kirk for Francis Larkin. After a mediocre first season, she would improve and in time become a winner. The other boat was Forcem (on the name see Appendix 1 to ch. I.1), which was built for a syndicate, whose most prominent partners were Edwin Schoettle and Ed Harrington. Again the builder was Kirk. The boat was disappointingly slow and would not compete the following year. On one account, called a rumor, the boat was scuttled in Toms River (*A Cats* p. 37). A different account reports that the boat was sold to a syndicate on Long Beach Island (an unnamed and undated newspaper article in the possession of Dan Crabbe). The latter seems more likely—once the boat had left upper Barnegat Bay, rumor could circulate freely—but reaching a firm conclusion is quite unimportant.

In 1924 still another A Cat joined the fleet. Frank Thacher found his first boat, Helen, too slow and decided to replace her with a new boat, Spy, which was built by Morton Johnson according to a Mower design. The decision seems to have been a sound one, for Spy would win the BBYRA season Championship in 1925 and again in 1927. Be that as it may, 1925 saw the last boat built by Morton Johnson according to a Mower design. That was Lotus. She was built for Bob Truit and would win the Sewell Cup in her first year. In the BBYRA Championship series, Lotus finished fourth behind Spy, Tamwock and Mary Ann but in front of Bat. For further details, see the BBYRA listing on the internet. And for Edward Luis Crabbe's account of the building boom, see below, Appendix 1 to ch. I.1.

Here a quasi-footnote may be in order. Above in the opening sentence, Mary Ann was referred to as "the first A Cat", being built in 1922. And it was said that in 1923 there was "a boom in building A Cats". Fair enough, but it is well to be clear that the label "A Cat" seems to have been coined or at least gained currency later in 1924, when the BBYRA recognized two classes of Catboats: A and B. On their architectural drawings, neither Mower nor Sweisguth use the label "A Cat". Rather they refer by name to the Mary Ann and to the Tamwock. Moreover, the BBYRA, in its internet list of winners for 1922 and 1923, recognizes a single class of Catboats. It is only later in the list of 1924 that the BBYRA recognizes two distinct classes. That agrees with handwritten lists in the possession of Dan Crabbe. These lists tell us that whereas in 1922 nine older boats competed against Mary Ann, in 1923 only a single older boat, Virginia, competed against the newer boats, now five in number. Apparently all but one of the owners of the older boats had been discouraged by Mary Ann's superior performance during the 1922 season. Accordingly, the owners decided overwhelmingly against futile competition. The BBYRA responded by creating two classes. In 1924 the newer boats raced together as A Cats, and the older boats were grouped together as B Cats. That change in classification may stand behind a confusion in "American Catboats" p. 101. There 1924 is cited as the year in which Mary Ann, Bat, Spy and Tamwock were built. But however the confusion is best explained, there is no strong reason to stop referring to Mary Ann as the first A Cat.

The handwritten lists possessed by Dan Crabbe are also of interest in that A Cat Helen is listed as a competitor not only in 1923 but also in 1924. Apparently Frank Thacher was pleased to be rid of Helen in 1924, but it does not follow that Helen raced only one year (*A Cats* p. 36). A photograph from 1924 shows Helen sailing together with Spy, Mary Ann and Bat (*A Cats* p. 7). In itself the photo is not proof of racing, but in combination with the handwritten list for 1924, there is strong reason to think that Helen raced that season. She appears at the bottom of the list with a measly nine points, which befits a slow boat. The question seems to be how often she was on the starting line.

Of greater interest is the assertion that Judge McKeehan's "sole purpose" in having Mary Ann built was to own a fast boat that would win the Tom's River Challenge Cup ("Beaton's *Ghost*" p. 20). Since Mary Ann was dominant in her first year—she won the Bay Championship in 1922—it is easy to imagine her winning the Cup in that year (*A Cats* p. 10-11, 140). But did she? Indeed, the Challenge Cup may not have been contested in 1922. The trophy records many winners, but for the years 1907 through 1922, it names no winners. And that is not exceptional: no winners are recorded for the years 1885, 1887-89, 1892, 1896-1904. Perhaps the race was not held in those years, including 1922.

In a chapter within Edwin Schoettle's *Sailing Craft*—it carries the title "The Toms River Cup"—Edward Crabbe describes the Cup as "famous" and asserts that the Cup "has been raced for by Catboats each year since 1871" (p. 367, cf. *A Cats* p. 9: "continuous competition"). Crabbe provides a lacunose list of winners based on the Cup and explains, "It is probable the Committee neglected to engrave the names of all the winners on the Cup. As no other record exists, it is impossible to state what boats won" (p. 374). Crabbe's caution is commendable. As someone who thinks of the Cup as famous (which it is among sailing buffs), he finds it unlikely that there were so many years in which the Cup was uncontested. But is it so unlikely—many yacht clubs have series, which fail and die or must be restarted. And is Crabbe's expression of ignorance concerning the years immediately preceding 1923 credible? He was one of the persons who was moved by Mary Ann's success to order an A Cat for the 1923 season, and he did so with Mower and Morton Johnson, the designer and builder of Mary Ann. He certainly knew who would have won the Cup in 1922, if the race had been held. And if McKeehan's motivation in commissioning Mary Ann was focused solely on winning the Challenge Cup, it is unlikely he would have allowed Mary Ann's victory in 1922 to go unrecorded. More likely winning the Challenge Cup would wait until 1923. It was Mary Ann's success over the entire summer of 1922—and that includes winning the BBYRA championship—that prompted a building boom aimed at the 1923 season. Mary Ann had demonstrated that the older boats could not compete successfully against the newcomer, which prompted the BBYRA to start a class especially for A Cats.

It is worth noting that Crabbe makes a connection between Mary Ann and an older boat named Gem. While most of the early boats that competed for the Challenge Cup were local to Barnegat Bay, Gem was brought to the Bay from Keyport, where she had been designed and built by Captain Bill Force. Her first race for the Challenge cup was 1881. She won in 1886 and again in 1893. Her last race for the cup was in 1923, when Crabbe restored her, both hull and spars, "thinking that she could do something against the modern Mower and Sweisguth catboats", but she was a failure. In racing for the Cup, Gem was defeated by Mary Ann ", and since then all the winners have been Marconi" (*Sailing Craft* p. 373). While not said explicitly, the implication is that 1923 saw a new beginning in competition for the Challenge Cup. Mary Ann had made her debut the year before, and her success helped restart and fundamentally change the level of competition.

A related concern is whether the A Cats started with a "Swedish" rig: that is, "with the main high on the hoist and a nine-foot gaff" (*A Cats* p.11, drawing on "American Catboats" p. 101). Here photographs are helpful. They show Bat, a Mower boat, and Forcem, a Sweisguth boat, both with a gaff (*A Cats* p. 30 and 37, respectively). Apparently in 1923, the two architects had boats on the water with a Swedish rig. In regard to Forcem, the photographic evidence is easily combined with surviving sail designs. There are two different designs drawn by Sweisguth, which make clear that in 1923 Tamwock—also a Sweisguth boat—started with a Swedish rig, and in 1924 switched to a Marconi rig (see ch. IV.1). Forcem would have gotten a Marconi rig in 1924, if she had not been scuttled or sold to people on Long Beach Island.

We have no sail plans for Bat, but a statement (apparently attributed to Alice Weber-Wright, *A Cats* p. 30) is suggestive. It runs, "The gaff on Bat was only used for a brief period of time." The statement has a conversational ring, so that it is probably a mistake to stress the adjective "brief". But if the statement can be taken at face value, one might suppose that Bat began the 1923 season with a Swedish rig, which was replaced by a Marconi rig early on during that season. Possible, but Tom Beaton reports that Edward Luis Crabbe (Edward's son, on whom see below, Appendix 1 to ch. I.1) was clear in stating that Bat did not get a Marconi rig until the following season. Like Tamwock, Bat sailed throughout 1923 with a Swedish rig. That seems more likely, but it invites a different question. Why did Bat ever have a Swedish rig? After all Mower's first A Cat, Mary Ann, had been designed and built with a Marconi rig. And it had been successful with that rig. Why, then, would a new Mower boat carry a different rig. An answer is ready at hand, as long as one keeps in mind that Bat was built for Edward Crabbe, who still believed in maintaining tradition. Indeed, he had Gem restored for the 1923 season including a "new mast and spars, and a new suit of sails" (*Sailing Craft* p. 373). We hear nothing of a change in type of rig, and there was none. Crabbe still believed that the Swedish rig could be a winner. We are not told how that thinking affected Bat. It is a guess but not unreasonable that Crabbe had Bat fitted with a Swedish rig, despite the fact that Mower's first A Cat, Mary Ann, had been successful with a Marconi rig. Bat was not altogether hopeless during 1923. In the BBYRA season championship, she finished second behind Mary Ann and in front of the two Sweisguth boats. In other words, she beat the other boats carrying a Swedish rig but not the proven winner with her Marconi rig. The remedy for Bat was to switch rigs for the 1924 season. Mower had it right from the beginning.

The idea that Mary Ann was built with and so always had a Marconi rig is, of course, incompatible with the view stated above: namely, the A Cats—the first being Mary Ann—began with a Swedish rig ("started" *A Cats* p. 11; "originally" in "American Catboats" p. 101). To be sure, there is no surviving photograph from 1922, showing Mary Ann sailing with a Marconi rig, but there is a Mower design possessed by Tom Beaton and shared with the Independence Seaport Museum in Philadelphia, which exhibits a Marconi rig, as does the design reproduced by Edwin Schoettle in his 1928 article on "American Catboats" (p. 94). The design is undated, so that someone might imagine a first design and then a second one: first a Swedish rig (1922) and then a Marconi rig (1923). But unless new evidence is brought to the table, the idea should be left aside. Too much imagination.

More important: the changing of rigs indicates that the A Cat class did not come into existence as a strict one-design class. Rather, from the beginning it was conceived of as a development class. Certain guidelines were recognized, e.g., the boats would be approximately 28 feet in length and 11 feet in width. But the limitations were loose. For minor variation in beam or width, see below fig. 2, Appendix 1 to ch. I.1. And for major variation, one need only consider variation in spars: first the Marconi rig (Mary Ann), then the Swedish rig (Bat, Tamwock, Forcem) and finally the Marconi rig for all A Cats. That is the way in which a development class evolves, and in the A Cat class the development of an efficient rig was not slow: by summer 1924, the Swedish rig had completely given way to the Marconi (see ch. IV.1 with figs. 87 and 88).

Fine and good, but from the beginning the A Cat class had attracted owners who wanted to win and most importantly could afford improvements in design and materials. That may be quite normal, but it can have a negative effect on camaraderie. Indeed, it encourages one to think of competitors as enemies. That may be overstatement, but Charles Mower's letter to Edward Crabb (on the spelling see below, Appendix 2 to ch. I) in January of 1923 is worthy of reflection. It is reproduced here:

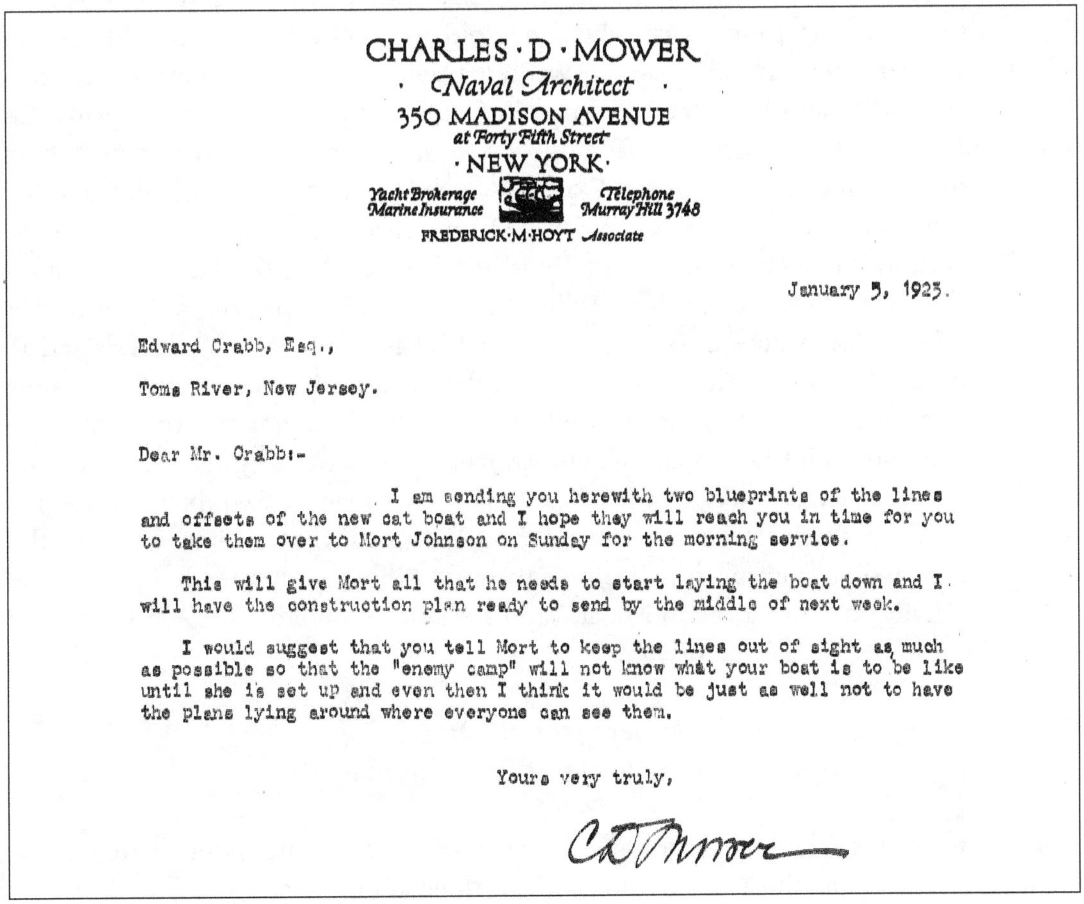

CHARLES · D · MOWER
· Naval Architect ·
350 MADISON AVENUE
at Forty Fifth Street
· NEW YORK ·
Yacht Brokerage   Telephone
Marine Insurance   Murray Hill 3748
FREDERICK · M · HOYT Associate

January 5, 1923.

Edward Crabb, Esq.,

Toms River, New Jersey.

Dear Mr. Crabb:-

   I am sending you herewith two blueprints of the lines and offsets of the new cat boat and I hope they will reach you in time for you to take them over to Mort Johnson on Sunday for the morning service.

   This will give Mort all that he needs to start laying the boat down and I will have the construction plan ready to send by the middle of next week.

   I would suggest that you tell Mort to keep the lines out of sight as much as possible so that the "enemy camp" will not know what your boat is to be like until she is set up and even then I think it would be just as well not to have the plans lying around where everyone can see them.

          Yours very truly,

          C D Mower

Fig. 1

Throughout the 1922 summer season, Mower had enjoyed success with Mary Ann, and now in January 1923 he realizes that he is not the only architect in the game. Being human, he wants to be on top and urges Crabb to instruct the builder to keep the plans for Bat out of sight, in order that they not be seen by the "enemy camp". Mower may be thinking of changes to the hull: in particular, the canoe-like bow that he designed for Bat. Being more vertical and not curved/sloping like that of Mary Ann, Bat's waterline would be lengthened, which might contribute to a gain in speed. In any case, Mower puts quotation marks around the phrase "enemy camp". Presumably, he is signaling overstatement, but "out of sight" is to be taken seriously. Over the years, changes deemed improvements would be made unannounced. (For an example, see ch. VI.2 on replacing wire with spectra.)

The depression of 1928 put a stop to the building of A Cats, so that when Tamwock was destroyed by fire in 1940, the number of A Cats was reduced to four: Mary Ann, Bat, Spy and Lotus (Helen and Forcem had already been rejected by their owners). All the surviving boats were suffering from neglect, so that after World War II, the class was in danger of going the way of the Dodo. That did not happen thanks to Nelson Hartranft, who took a liking to A Cats and decided to save the class. He bought the surviving four boats, which he sold for modest sums to others, who would maintain them. In addition, he wanted David Beaton and Sons—affectionately known as "Beaton's"—to build a new A Cat, but the whereabouts of plans was quite unknown. That changed when a set of Sweisguth's plans was discovered in an antique store on Route 9 in Ocean County. Lachlan, "Lally," Beaton, who was the son of David and at the time president of Beaton's, agreed to undertake the project. In 1980 Wasp was launched thereby adding a fifth boat to the fleet. Beaton's went on to rebuild Spy in 1984 and Lotus in 1986. While that was going on, Mary Ann was rebuilt in Brooklin, Maine at Benjamin River Marine, and Bat was fiberglassed in Bob Lostrom's shop in the Amboys. The A Cat fleet had been rescued, and more new boats would be built. In 1987 Peter Kellogg had John Brady at the Independence Seaport Museum build Tamwock, which was named after the original Tamwock but unlike the original was based on a Mower design. That made a sixth boat competing in the annual summer series sponsored by the BBYRA. Five years later in 1992, Bill Fortenbaugh would commission Beaton's to build Ghost, and Peter Kellogg would ask John Brady to build a second boat, Vapor. When completed, these boats would bring the number of A Cats to eight.

Appendix 1 to ch. I.1
The Account of E. L. Crabbe

The details of the building boom are reported in several sources and therefore are treated succinctly in the present book. Nevertheless, one account of the boom is largely unknown and is reproduced here, for it was written by Edward Luis Crabbe, the son of Edward Crabbe (no middle name), who commissioned the building of Bat but probably never raced her. That is the judgment of Daniel Church McEwen Crabbe (Dan), who is the grandson of Edward, son of Daniel McEwen Crabbe and nephew of Edward Luis Crabbe. According to Dan, his uncle and his father were 22 and 20 years old, respectively, when Bat was built, and they will have raced the newly built boat. One might expect the account of Edward Luis to be authoritative, but it is curiously faulty. The account runs as follows:

CLASS A CATBOATS

The Barnegat Bay A cats differ from the traditional catboats in that they are marconi rigged. They were designated A cats to distinguish them from traditional cats, B cats, by the BBYRA.

The first A cat was Mary Ann. She was so successful, a class was formed and four new boats built the following year.

All A cats are 28'04 about 22'Beam and 2'6"Draft. Masts are about 45'. The first few years they were given time allowances but were so evenly matched, they raced boat for boat thereafter. All are now marconi rigged but the Bat, Tamwock, Helen and Foresome had a 6' gaff at the mast head, the Sweedish rig, when built. This did not work out, and at the end of the season the gaff was eliminated and the sails recut.

THE FLEET

Mary Ann 1922 Designed by Charles D. Mower, Built by Morton Johnson, Bay Head, for Judge McKean IHYC. Still sailing.

Bat 1923 Designed by Mower, built by Johnson for Edward Crabbe, TRYC. Still sailing.

Tamwock 1923 Designed by Francis Sweisguth, Built by John Kirk, Toms River For F. P. Larkin SPYC. Burned in boatyard fire in 1940s.

Foresome 1923 Designed by Sweisguth, built by Kirk for syndicate headed by Edwin J. Schoettle IHYC. Not successful. Raced only one year.

Helen 1923 Designed by Mower, Built Hoppers Basin Seaside Park, for Frank Thatcher, SHYC . Not successful. Raced only one year.

Spy 1924 Designed by Mower, Built by Johnson for Frank Thatcher, to replace Helen. Still sailing.

Lotus 1924 Designed by Mower, Built by Johnson for J. P. Truitt,Jr, IHYC. Still around. raced until three years ago.

These are the A cats that have raced on Barnegat Bay for sixty years. All have had many owners, and except for the two unsuccessful designs, each has won her share of major challenge cup races and BBYRA championships.

Edward L. Crabbe
March 25 1962

Fig. 2

As indicated in the penultimate line, the above account was written by Edward L = Luis Crabbe, who was born in July of 1902 and died at the age of 87 in May of 1990. He was well educated—Berkshire School and Princeton University—but had such poor penmanship that what he wrote was often illegible. That may explain some of the errors or confusions in the account printed here. The clearest example is reporting the beam or width of an A Cat as 22 feet. That is off by some 11 feet, which suggests that something has fallen out. Most likely we should supply "Length" after "28" and "Waterline Length" after "22". Before "Beam" we should supply a measurement like "11", which approximates the width of Mary Ann. Bat is 10 ½ feet wide, and according to Sweisguth's design (the scale is 1 inch = 1 foot), Tamwock will have measured c. 10 ½ feet at its widest point (see ch. II.2 figs. 8 and 11), which is the width of both Ghost and Raven, also built according to Sweisguth's design. Since Edward had poor penmanship, we can easily imagine someone else typing up his account. Being unable to make out certain words and pressed for time, the typist decided to omit what was illegible. The false starts/cancellations after "28" are likely to reflect hesitation, after which the typist jumped ahead. That is, of course, no more than a guess, but positing a lacuna is by no means foolish.

A further difficulty is the statement that the A Cats have been racing on Barnegat Bay "for sixty years". That should date the account to 1983, but the date at the bottom of the account seems to tell otherwise. Almost certainly the typist wrote 1962, after which the typist or someone else wrote over the six. If the correction is compared with the correction some seven lines above where a "5" replaces a "4", one is tempted to say that the date of the account is corrected to read 1952. But that is uncertain, and Dan prefers to see "8" replacing "6" at the bottom of the account. That is not impossible for Edward Luis was still alive in 1982. Moreover, it explains the assertion that the A Cats had been racing for sixty years: fifty-nine was rounded off to sixty. In addition, the recent launching of Wasp in 1980 is likely to have stimulated interest in the building of the earliest A Cats. Edward Luis responded with the account printed here.

The phrase "Sweedish rig" is a simple error for "Swedish rig." The rig—a short gaff on a tall mast—was much in use in Sweden and generally in Scandinavian waters during the beginning of the twentieth century, and for that reason acquired the name "Swedish rig". The spelling error in Edward Luis' account may have been caused by the vagaries of English spelling. Since "sweet" is spelled with a double "e", why not "Sweedish" instead of "Swedish". That said, one hates to attribute such an error to a Princeton graduate. Surely the phantom typist is to blame.

Finally, there are two proper names that merit comment. One is "Thacher" which is twice misspelled with a second "t". That error recurs in modern accounts, with one notable exception. On the internet, "Thacher" appears in the BBYRA Championship results for the years 1923 to 1927. Again, blame the typist.

The other proper name is "Foresome". Here too we have an error. The name is used in reference to an A Cat built in 1923, but the correct name of that boat is "Forcem". According to Suzy Davis, the granddaughter of Edwin Schoettle, "Forcem" is most likely a deliberate misspelling, being a phonetic rendering of "Foursome". It plays on the fact that the owners of the boat formed a syndicate composed of four persons". One of the four was T. A. Daly, who was a reporter, poet and humorist; he may have named the boat. Perhaps then Edward Luis was trying to unpack the name Forcem, but instead of writing "Foursome", he erred and wrote "Foresome". One hesitates to blame the typist for still another error.

Appendix 2 to ch. I.1
Mower's Letter to Crabb

The letter from Charles Mower to Edward Crabb is a precious document, which is now in the possession Dan Crabbe, Edward's grandson (see fig. 1). The omission of the "e" on the end of Edward's last name is not a typo; rather it is part of the Crabbe family history. The final "e" goes back to the family's roots in South Western England. Like the German "Krabbe", the common noun "crabbe" refers to the edible crustacean that is found along most seacoasts. As often the common noun became a family name through association with a particular form of work, here the gathering of crustaceans. When Dan's great great grandfather immigrated to Cuba, he dropped the "e" because the "e" is not pronounced in English, but was pronounced by the people of Cuba. Later at the age of 9, Dan's great grandfather left Cuba for America. The family name remained the same until his children restored the "e" late in the nineteenth century, but the restoration needed time to take hold. In the letter by Mower to Edward, the shortened form recurs.

In the second paragraph, the phrase "laying the boat down" refers to lofting, on which see ch. II.3.1. In the second and third paragraphs, "Mort" is short, familiar for Morton.

2. Why Ghost ?

The question "Why Ghost?" has been put to Bill Fortenbaugh on numerous occasions, but not always for the same reason. The first and most common reason is puzzlement: Why would Bill choose to have Beaton's build an old fashioned boat that no one in 1992 would describe as high performance. In recent years, Bill had been racing M Scows and E Scows, both of which are challenging boats, which in a blow on downwind legs lift out of the water and skim across the surface. Why should he prefer a boat that is considerably slower and so heavy that lifting out of the water is never in question? Even when the wind approaches 20, all competitors plow along at hull speed. The oddity here is understandable, but it also suggests an answer. Bill was in his late fifties and realized that he had not only lost half a step (called aging) but also and more importantly was so immersed in Aristotelian and Theophrastean Studies (called a professor's life) that there was no time to practice. Skipper and crew needed to find time to get their act together, and that seemed out of reach. A closely related consideration follows from the first: tipping over in heavy wind had occurred too many times. To be sure, Bill enjoyed the exhilaration of planing downwind with spinnaker up, but that is a pleasure normally reserved for a practiced crew. A desideratum that seemed unattainable. Moreover, Bill had grown up sailing old fashioned boats: the twelve foot Duck Boat, which acquired its name from its roots in duckhunting, the fifteen foot Sneakbox, which at the time was made by J. H. Perrine in Barnegat, and the nineteen foot G Sloop which was made by Morton Johnson. During the 1940s and early 1950s, when Bill was still a tyro, all three boats were sailed with the skipper steering, while a different person trimmed the sail. Dividing duties in this way would remain the norm in boats with large mainsails. The A Cat is a paradigm. But a boat like the E Scow is different: the skipper both steers and trims the mainsail. Ideally that provides better control and hence better boat speed. But it also demands coordination and a measure of strength, especially when jibing in heavy air. Bill was conscious of slippage in these areas and saw in the A Cat a way to avoid trimming a sail while steering.

Finally a very different consideration, an aesthetic one, would be decisive. During the summer of 1992, Bill had more than once observed the A Cats starting a race. Clustered together with c. 47 foot masts and 28 foot booms supporting a massive mainsail, the boats were not only awesome but also beautiful. And that beauty became so attractive as to be irresistible. Only a week or two after the last race of the BBYRA season, an order was placed at Beaton's. Such promptness turned out to be good fortune, for Peter Kellogg, who had already had one A Cat, Tamwock, built at the Independence Seaport Museum in Philadelphia and had recently become disappointed in the boat's performance, decided to have a second boat built. Peter went to Beaton's and asked Tom, Lally's son and now president of the company, whether he would build the boat. The inquiry was sensible, but the timing was poor, for Tom had already committed to building Ghost. As a result, Peter returned to Philadelphia and put his request to John Brady, who responded positively. He would build Vapor, and like Peter he had speed on his mind. Hence, in 1994 two new A Cats would be racing and inevitably enjoying a friendly rivalry, which would peak two years later in 1996 (see ch. V.2).

Still a different reason for asking "Why Ghost?" is that the name Ghost is rarely seen on the transom of a boat, large or small, motor or sail. One might guess that Bill was haunted by images of A Cats before and after placing an order at Beaton's—the guess finds some support in a cartoon that Bill drew in order to celebrate thirty-five years of marriage in 1994 (see fig. 3)—but the truth is different. The name was suggested by John Dickson, who crewed on Bill's E Scow and would follow him to Ghost (ch. VIII.2). During the period when Ghost was being constructed, Bill was at a loss to come up with an appropriate name. He could do no better than "Slow Poke" or "Retiree". Then one day in conversation with John, Bill broached the topic of a suitable name and observed that three existing A Cats had threatening names of one syllable: "Bat" (scary at night), "Spy" (furtive and hostile) and "Wasp" (a formidable sting). John immediately responded with "Ghost". A perfect fit, which would be spelled out on the transom and signaled above on the sail with a large "G", colored dark green to match the hull (ch. III.1). Threatening names have never become a class rule, but three boats built subsequently did adopt such a name: "Witch" (ugly sorcerer) 2000, "Raven" (rapacious omnivore) 2001 and "Spyder" (spider) 2008.

Fig. 3

II
BUILDING GHOST

1. The Woodshop

Fig. 4

Ghost was constructed at David Beaton and Sons, located in Brick NJ at the end of Beaton Road and across Barnegat Bay from the Borough of Mantoloking. More precisely, the construction took place in the main shed, commonly referred to as the woodshop, which is shown here in fig. 4. We see the western side of the shop; the eastern side looks out on the Bay.

Some thirteen years earlier, Wasp had been built in the woodshop. At that time Lally Beaton was in charge; his son Tom worked with him. Subsequently Spy and Lotus were rebuilt in the same building, and in 1993 Ghost followed. Lally had now stepped aside, so that Tom directed the project, working together with Paul Smith, who had long worked at Beaton's and had participated in building Wasp and in re-building Spy and Lotus. Joining Tom and Paul was Russ Manheimer, who had been working in insurance before turning to boat building. Later he would return to in-surance, but during the construction of Ghost, he worked alongside Tom and Paul.

Past experience had demonstrated that the woodshop was large enough for build-ing Ghost. The main room measures approximately 50 feet by 29. An A Cat is roughly 28 feet long and 11 feet wide. "Plenty of space" the layman is apt to say, but in fact builders need space to move around a boat under construction. In addition, they need sufficient floor space for building materials like large planks, before they are attached to the hull. Also needed are benches for the tools and diagrams that are es-sential to the building process. To be sure, there was an extension to the woodshop on the northwest side. It was large enough to handle special projects such as making the rudder and tiller for Ghost, but that space was also needed for quite unrelated projects. However important building Ghost may have been, there were other boats that needed attention, some of which belonged to loyal customers, who looked to Beaton's for quality care.

Fig. 5

Fig. 6

A special consideration was the onset of winter. There would be cold weather and the woodshop did not have the luxury of a modern heating system: one that surrounded the room with baseboard piping, through which hot water circulated, or with well placed air-vents that doubled for heat in the winter and cool air in the summer. Rather it depended on a single oil furnace in the northeast corner and two wood-fired stoves in the southwest corner. The two stoves are shown in fig. 5. On the right we see a basic woodstove. It is seen from the side. The large pipe on top removes the smoke that is generated by burning wood. *Re vera*, the stove seen in the photo is a replacement, but the size and position duplicate that which was in use during the winters of 1992-93 and 93-94.

The stove to the left was present when Ghost was built and is still in place today. Functionally it is a boiler, which creates steam to facilitate bending wood such as the white oak that would become ribs (ch. II.3) and the mahogany that would become the sides of Ghost's cabin (ch. II.5). The large pipe behind the boiler removes smoke. The smaller pipe which is joined to the boiler at its top carries steam (moist heat) to the long box in which wood is placed and steamed before it is bent. That box can be seen in the upper left of fig. 5. The actual join to the box takes place a foot or so outside the photo. A second smaller pipe can be seen to the right of the boiler. It is attached to the long box and returns condensed steam to the boiler for reheating.

The long box is seen clearly in fig. 6. It begins within the woodshop and extends outside the shop in order to accommodate long planks such as the white cedar planks which will be bent as they are attached to ribs and made to form the sides of Ghost. The box is covered with a synthetic material that protects the box from weather and helps insulate the box when it is filled with steam.

Both stoves were fired with split logs and scraps of wood left over from various projects. To the outsider that sounds quite romantic, but a woodstove requires attention. Left to burn through the night without additional fuel, the fire is likely to go out so that it must be rekindled at the start of the next day. Pesty perhaps, but with few exceptions the two stoves in combination with the oil furnace were adequate for keeping warm Tom, Paul, Russ and others, whose efforts over two winters put together A Cat Ghost.

Fig. 7

Another beneficiary of the wood burning stoves was Bozo the cat, who would find a comfortable spot and overlook the work as Ghost took shape. In the photo, he is shown on a chair with a cushion just thick enough to be comfortable. From this position Bozo watched the skeleton of ribs and cross beams being assembled and later the construction of the finished boat: one that was planked and fitted out with deck and cabin. Throughout it all, the mouser kept vigil. That is, until his eyes began to close (fig. 7) and sleep set in (see ch.III.1 figs. 82 and 83).

2. Two Sweisguth Plans: the Hull

At the beginning of this book (ch. I.1), reference was made to Francis Sweisguth, who designed Tamwock for Francis Larkin. Tamwock was destroyed by fire and for years Sweisguth's plans were missing. When they were subsequently found in an antique shop, they were used in building Wasp for Nelson Hartranft. These same plans would be used again when Ghost was built. There were plans for the hull, including deck, centerboard and rudder as well as plans for sails and spars. The latter, i.e., Sweisguth's plans for sails and spars, will be printed and discussed in a later chapter (ch. IV.1). Here the plans for the hull are under consideration. There are three drawings or designs, two of which are dated to March 1923 and a third to November 1923. The March pair are printed at the end of this section on facing pages (figs. 8 and 9). The November design and the table of offsets composed for that design—it is dated October 31— are also printed at the end of this section on facing pages (figs. 10 and 11).

The first of the two March plans (fig. 8) focuses on the hull proper, bottom and topsides, which are pictured from underneath and from the side. The plan details the curvature of the hull and shows the position of the deadwood, rudder and centerboard (on which see ch. II.3 and 6). Of especial interest are the solid and broken lines that appear in close proximity to each other on the forward half of the hull. Sweisguth himself calls attention to the lines. On the plan underneath the side view, he writes "solid lines show new waterlines" and "dotted (lines show) old (waterlines)". Apparently Sweisguth is calling attention to a change in design. For the summer season of 1923, he had drawn plans for two boats: Forcem and Tamwock (see ch. I.1). The older lines are for Forcem and speak for a lean, sloped bow. The new lines are for Tamwock and call for a fuller, blunter bow.

The second March plan (fig. 9 on the right-hand page) focuses on structural details. The boat is pictured from above and from the side. The ribbing is presented in detail: the individual ribs number forty both in the hull and under the deck. The locations of the mast and the side stays are clearly marked; similarly, the location of the cabin and cockpit within the deck is made clear. The same may be said of the steel straps that in the front of the boat run from side to side and in the rear run from side to transom. Forward on the starboard side the straps are represented by broken lines. That indicates that the straps will not be seen when the decking is completed. They will be set into the upper surface of the deck beams, after which planks will be laid down and covered with canvas. At least that is how decking in Tamwock and Wasp proceeded. In the case of Ghost, the decking was made of plywood covered with xynole (see ch. II.5.3).

Before leaving the second March plan, it should be noted that the interior of the cabin area is left uncovered on the port side. That reveals an omission: namely, the absence of a toilet in the area immediately within the cabin alongside the partition that separates the cockpit from the cabin. In contrast, Mower's design of Mary Ann exhibits a toilet in that position. The inclusion makes good sense, for on Barnegat Bay the cruising type of catboat was "still in vogue for (both) racing and cruising" ("American Catboats" p. 95, 101). Nevertheless, Sweisguth omits the toilet. To be sure a toilet could be added later, but most likely Sweisguth knows that his customers are primarily interested in racing and accordingly omits amenities appropriate to cruising.

The November plan (fig. 10) repeats the focus on the bottom of the boat and its curvature. Now the broken or dotted lines are gone. Tamwock was built according to the "new" lines, which are reproduced without comment. That is most likely correct, but if so the two-line notice in the bottom right hand corner of the plan is puzzling. There we read in the first line "new fore-body", and in a second line immediately below the first, "built Nov. 1923". At first reading, one is tempted to understand that the new fore-body was built during the late fall of 1923. I.e., the forward part of the hull was rebuilt, so as to be fuller. We might imagine that Francis Larkin was disappointed in finishing the BBYRA summer series in third place behind not only Mary Ann but also Bat, which like Tamwock was built in the spring of 1923. To be sure, Tamwock did beat two other new boats: namely, Forcem, which was built for Edwin Schoettle, and Helen, which was built for Frank Thacher. But these boats were deemed hopelessly slow and replaced by their owners: Thacher had Spy built and Schoettle had Lotus built. Perhaps Larkin's response to disappointment was more measured. He had the forward part of the existing hull rebuilt. Possible, but there is no good evidence to support such an explanation. A more likely explanation is suggested by the November 1923 sail plan (see ch. IV.1). After the summer racing season in 1923, Sweisguth designed a new sail and rig, mast and boom, for Tamwock: the original Swedish rig with its gaff was replaced by a Marconi rig. That prompted Sweisguth to redraw the hull plan omitting the dotted lines that were not followed in building Tamwock. The date November 1923 is correct for the new drawing, but "built" is an unfortunate slip.

More important: choosing the unbroken lines—the new lines that determined the shape of Tamwock's fore-body—most likely had consequences for the racecourse, not only in the 1920s but also later in the century when new A Cats were built. In 1980 Beaton's built Wasp according to Sweisguth's new lines and some 14 years later did the same in building Ghost. The new lines call for a fuller bow, which may explain, at least in part, Ghost's success downwind in heavy air. A fuller, blunter bow—one that is more perpendicular to the water—enters the water sooner, and therefore displaces more water up front. It is more buoyant and less likely to plow water. But with this gain comes a negative. When sailing upwind in heavy air and a rolling sea, a leaner bow is likely to cut through the waves with greater ease, and when coming about it may minimize the seemingly inevitable loss in forward momentum. That may explain some of Ghost's difficulties upwind in heavy air (on Ghost and Mary

Ann dueling, see ch. VII.2), but it must not be forgotten that the hand on the tiller plays an important role.

The offset table (fig. 11) presents a series of measurements that are likely to confuse a person who has never worked with, let alone seen, such a table. But to the builder they are not only intelligible but of great importance. For they make it possible to construct a hull that is identical on both sides: i.e., port and starboard exhibit the same curvature at the same point when measured from the centerline. And that line is fixed by a wire stretched tight above and a duplicate line drawn below (see II.3.1 on preliminaries). As an example of how to read the table, station no. 7 may be selected. It can be seen in figs. 8 and 10, where it marks the widest point of the boat. The table tells us that at WL, which is 12 inches above LWL (the "load waterline", which may be explained as the actual waterline when the boat is rigged and afloat), the half breadth or width is 5 feet, 2 inches and 3 eighths. Multiplied by 2, the total width is 10 feet, 4 inches and 6 eighths. Since WL approaches but does not reach the top of the hull, which is slightly wider than the width at WL, we can say that the measurement given in the table is very much in line with Sweisguth's March design (fig. 8), of which the scale is said to be 1 inch = 1 foot. When the design is measured at its widest point, i.e. at station no. 7, the distance across the entire hull is 10 ½ inches, which translates into 10 feet six inches.

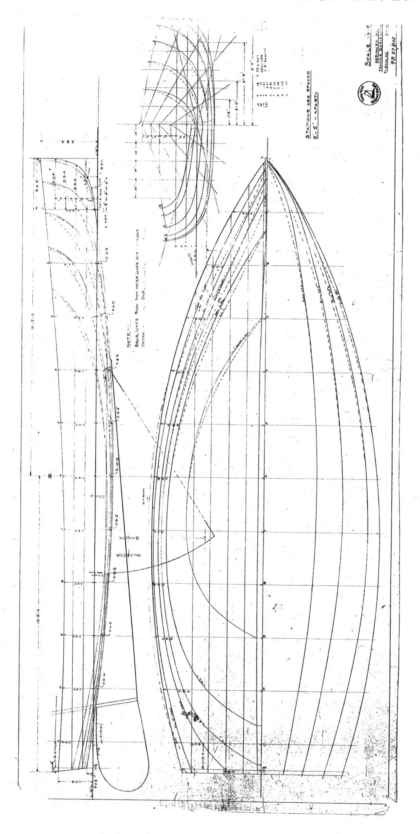

Fig. 8

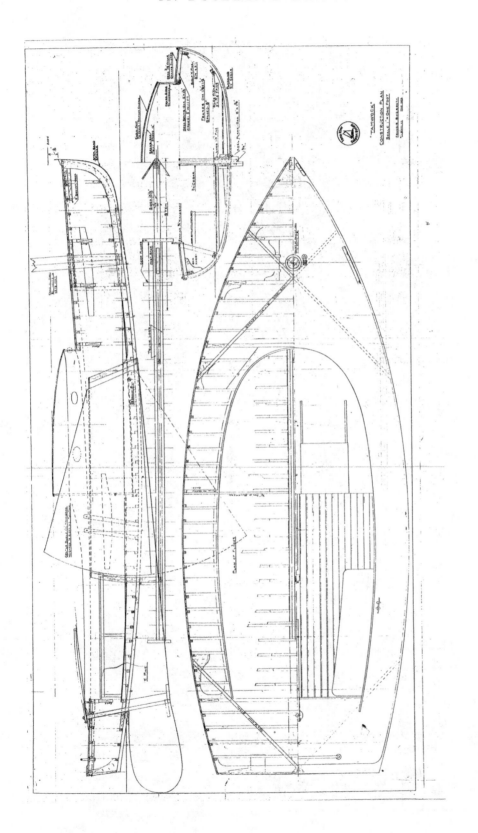

Fig. 9

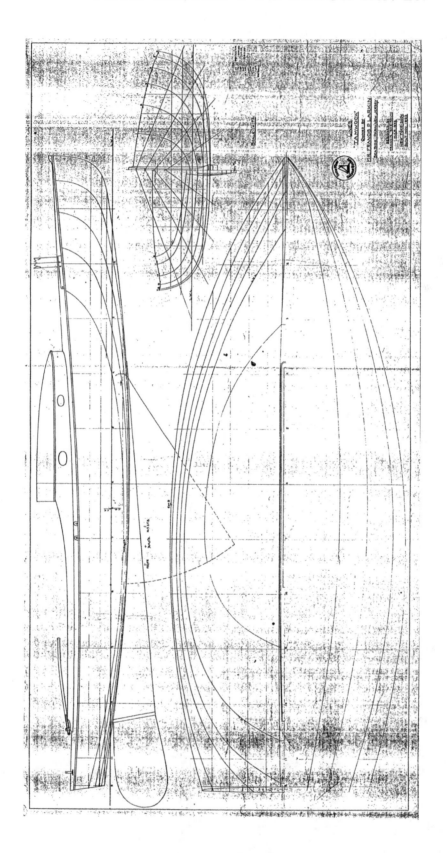

Fig. 10

OFFSET TABLE FOR NEW BOW FOR "TAMWOCK"

DIMENSIONS ARE IN FEET-INCHES AND EIGHTHS OF INCHES

THE BASE LINE IS THE L.W.L.

MEASUREMENTS FOR HEIGHTS FROM BASE LINE UP AND DEPTHS FROM BASE LINE DOWN

STATIONS ARE **2 FT. 5 INCHES APART**

BREADTHS, CENTER LINE OUT

WATER LINES ARE 6" APART

BUTTOCK LINES ARE 10-20-30-40-INCHES OUT FROM CENTER LINE

ALL MEASUREMENTS ARE TO OUTSIDE OF PLANK

THICKNESS OF PLANKING - 3/4"

STEM SIDED 3½" WITH 3/4" FACE AT L.W.L. TO 2" AT HEAD.

FRANCIS SWEISGUTH
Pt. Dept. Room 981.
OCT. 30 1923.

98.078.01

STATIONS	1	2	3	4	5	6	7	8	9	10	11	11½
HALF BREADTHS FROM CENTER LINE on W.L. 12" ABOVE L.W.L.	1-2-7	2-5-0	3-5-1	4-2-6	4-9-2	5-1-0	5-2-3	5-1-7	4-11-4	4-6-2	3-10-1	3-4-4
" 6" "	0-10-0	1-11-6	3-0-5	3-10-7	4-6-0	4-10-2	5-0-0	4-11-2	4-7-7	4-1-0	2-10-2	1-8-4
ON LOAD WATER LINE		1-0-7	2-4-3	3-4-3	4-0-6	4-5-6	4-7-3	4-6-2	4-0-1	2-7-2		
" 6" BELOW L.W.L.				2-0-9	3-0-2	3-6-0	3-7-2	2-1-7				
HALF BREADTHS FROM CENTER LINE OUT ON DIAGONAL No 1	1-8-0	2-10-5	3-9-4	4-6-1	5-0-1	5-3-3	5-5-0	5-4-3	5-2-0	4-9-2	4-2-2	3-10-2
" 2	1-7-3	2-7-7	3-5-3	4-0-7	4-6-2	4-9-3	4-10-2	4-5-1	4-5-9	3-11-6	3-3-6	2-11-6
" 3	1-5-4	2-2-6	2-9-6	3-3-1	3-6-5	3-8-1	3-8-0	3-6-2	3-2-9	2-9-2	2-2-6	1-11-4
" 4	1-1-1	1-6-7	1-11-5	2-2-7	2-4-7	2-5-4	2-5-1	2-3-6	2-0-6	1-8-3	1-3-4	1-1-0
HEIGHTS AND DEPTHS ABOVE AND BELOW L.W.L. ON BUTTOCK 10" OUT FROM CENTER LINE	ABOVE 0-6-0	BELOW 0-0-7	BELOW 0-5-1	0-7-7	0-9-3	0-9-6	0-9-4	0-8-1	0-5-5	BELOW 0-2-2	ABOVE 0-2-1	0-4-4
HEIGHTS AND DEPTHS 20"	ABOVE 0-3-2	ABOVE 0-0-7	0-3-1	0-6-7	0-8-6	0-9-3	0-9-1	0-7-7	0-5-1	BELOW 0-1-3	0-3-3	0-5-7
" 30"	1-1-1	ABOVE 0-0-7	0-5-7	BELOW 0-4-5	0-7-4	0-8-4	0-8-2	0-7-0	0-5-4	BELOW 0-0-1	0-5-3	0-8-7
" 40"		0-5-7		0-0-2	0-4-7	0-6-5	0-6-0	0-5-4	0-2-4	0-1-6	6-8-0	0-11-6

Fig. 11

3. Framing, Planking, and Decking

Although the heading to this section mentions three important stages in the building of an A Cat, the process is more complex. Accordingly the section will be divided into five units: 1) Preliminaries that prepare for the actual construction, i.e., that are accomplished prior to the fitting and joining together of the component parts, 2) The Core Structure of the boat: the keel, deadwood, bedlogs, headledges, maststep, stem and transom 3) Framing and Planking the Hull, 4) Preparing for the Deck, and 5) The Deck in Place.

1) Preliminaries

Each of the major component parts of an A Cat is made from patterns taken from full size drawings created during what is called the lofting process. The name "lofting" comes from the fact that typically the creation of patterns is not accomplished on the floor on which the boat will be built. Rather the patterns are made elsewhere, such as a loft above the work area. Hence, the name "lofting". More important, each of the structural parts must be made in strict accordance with the patterns, in both shape and size. For any inadvertent deviation will create serious difficulties as the parts are assembled.

Perhaps obvious, but for clarity's sake it is well to add that the process of lofting need not be repeated for each new boat built to the same design. That is true in regard to Ghost. Beaton's had already built Wasp, and in preparation for that boat Lally had spent months in the loft above the woodshop making patterns for building Wasp. After that boat had been built, these patterns were stored away and brought out for use in building Ghost. Indeed, they would be used twice again, when Raven and Lightning were built.

In addition to making new or reusing old patterns, the construction process greatly benefits from the placement of centerlines above and on the floor where the work will take place. The line above the work area takes the form of a wire stretched tight fore and aft near the ceiling. Vertical plumb lines are dropt from this line, which makes it possible to mark a duplicate line on the floor directly underneath the wire above. Each part of the internal structure can then be centered and set in a vertical position in accordance with either the upper or lower centerlines. The same holds for the deadwood. The lower line on the floor also acts as a horizontal base line for measuring the width of the whole, the sides (port and starboard) and distances in between. These distances are listed in the table of offsets (see above, ch. 2.2 fig. 11). A lopsided boat does not win races.

Like the patterns produced in lofting, the upper and lower centerlines used in building Wasp were at least in principle reusable in constructing another boat. In the case of Ghost, that was true of the upper centerline. It was still in place some thirteen years later. The line drawn on the floor, however, would have been lost through wear and tear, but in fact it was lost when a new plywood floor was put down replacing an older floor made of planks. That replacement was an improvement, smoother for working on and easier to mark up with a carpenter's pencil . The process of producing the lower centerline remained the same: it involved hanging plumb lines from the wire above at several different locations.

For an illustration of a plumb line in use, see below ch. II.3.3 fig. 20. The plumb is visible between two molds, which tells us that the construction of Ghost had already progressed well beyond preliminaries.

2) The Core Structure of Ghost

Fig. 12

The actual building of Ghost started with the core, which finds its place in the middle or more accurately along the centerline of the boat. Seven distinct components may be picked out: the keel, bedlogs, headledges, deadwood, the maststep, the bow piece or stem and the transom.

Caveat: the photo printed above (fig. 12) is exceptional in that it is not of Ghost but of her sister ship Raven. No photo of Ghost at this stage in the building process could be found, so that a photo of Raven has been introduced. All other photos illustrating the building process are of Ghost.

In the photo, the stem is the most forward part. Below it joins the keel, which is made from a single plank of mahogany. The keel runs the length of the boat, approximately 26 feet from stem to transom. It is 9 inches wide and 1 7/8 inches thick. At the end it joins the transom, which in the photo is not yet attached. Sweisguth's March design calls for an oak keel (ch. II.2 fig. 9), but in building Ghost, Beaton's opted for mahogany among the available planks. Oak would be used on later boats, i.e., on Raven and Lightning.

While work is being done on the core, it is supported by horses, which create a convenient height for working on the whole. Later when the core has been completed and work begins on framing, the horses will be replaced by more stable supports: e.g., the three-legged support seen near the stem on the far side of the core structure.

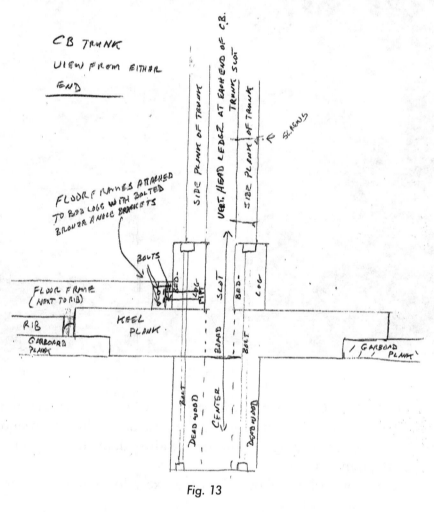

Fig. 13

On both sides of the keel, the bottom half was cut into and reduced in width: i.e., while the upper half, which will be facing into the boat and visible in the bilge, was left intact, the width of the lower portion, which would be facing outside the boat and visible to fish and crabs, was shortened. As a result, the shape of the keel resembles the letter "T", albeit a very squat "T". That allows the "garboard" plank, the lowest plank of the hull, to overlap the keel on the bottom half. See Paul Smith's drawing: the keel plank which extends horizontally to the right and to the left, is cut in such a way that it accepts the garboard plank on both sides (fig. 13).

In addition, an opening or slot 1 1/2 inches wide and 8 feet 10 inches long was cut into the middle of the keel. That was to become the opening for the "centerboard, which is 1 ¼ inches in width." Construction of the "well" or "trunk" (see ch. II.6.1), which would rise above the opening and through which the centerboard would be lowered and raised, began with "bedlogs", i.e., the two widest and lowest side-pieces, which are made of mahogany. These pieces are slightly curved on the bottom and contribute to giving Ghost's hull its proper shape. Later additional sidepieces would be added, so that the well reached its appointed height.

Fig. 14

Fore and aft, the opening of the well was closed with "headledges": a strait piece of white oak in the front and a curved piece in the rear. The latter matches the curve of the rear edge of the centerboard. In fig. 14, the curve of the rear headledge is seen rising out of and above the bedlogs.

Fig. 15

Below the keel, a construct of layered pieces of mahogany finds its place (fig. 15). It is called "deadwood" and runs from the forward end of the opening for the centerboard to the rudder at the rear of the boat. The deadwood is made with an opening through which the centerboard can move up and down. Behind the opening, the deadwood is solid and becomes deeper as it progresses aft. The deadwood ends with a vertical board, into which the rudderpost will be fitted at a later time. See the designs of Sweisguth (figs. 8 and 10) as well as the photo fig. 15. In the photo, atop the keel and toward the end of the deadwood, one sees floor frames, which belong to a later step: they will be permanently attached when framing begins. (See below, Section 3 with fig. 21.)

For clarity's sake, it may be noted that the rear of the deadwood is not to be confused with the skeg of a boat. The latter is not a part of a larger construct but rather an independent piece in the rear of a boat. It is well known to sailors of small boats like Lightnings and Comets. Nevertheless, a skeg and the rear of the deadwood are similar in function. They not only provide support for the rudder but also make steering easier. That is especially true in an A Cat, whose weather helm in heavy air is countered to some extent by the size of the deadwood in the rear of the boat (on the centerboard countering weather helm, see ch. II.6.1).

The term "deadwood" is not in everyone's vocabulary, and in any case it is an oddity. Most likely it reflects the fact that the layered mahogany attached to the keel has no moving parts and so might be referred to as lifeless or dead.

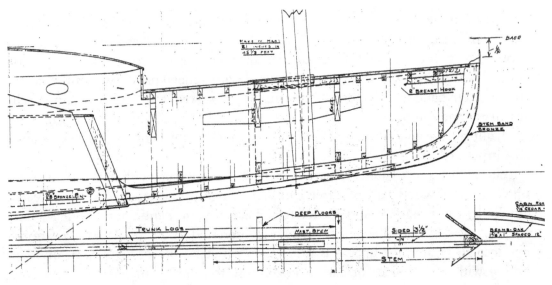

Fig. 16

Turning now to the maststep: it finds its place toward the front of the boat between the bedlogs and the stem. It is a single piece of heavy oak suitable for supporting a c. 48 foot mast and resisting the pressure created by stays pulled tight. Fig. 16 is a detail taken from Sweisguth's March design (fig. 9). It well illustrates the position of the maststep, but not the way in which Ghost's maststep is integrated into the core structure. See below, end of this section, item 4.

Fig. 17

Fig. 17 (on the preceeding page) shows the stem of Ghost up close. On both sides of the stem, a rabbet is cut in, so that side planks coming forward can be attached smoothly, i.e. without creating unnecessary turbulence at the very front of the boat. Later the forward face of the stem will be fitted with a metal plate. Sweisguth's design calls for a stem band made of bronze (see fig. 16). It serves as protection against collisions, major and minor alike. In addition it extends slightly above stem and functions as a chainplate to which the forestay is attached. Ghost was fitted out with such a dual-purpose band.

It should be noted that in 1980 when Beaton's built Wasp, the stem was made from a single piece of wood, part of a tree trunk, in which the upward curve was created naturally by the passage from root to stem. That has a romantic appeal—it recalls a time gone by—but for the craftsman who is interested in creating a strong, smooth entry into the water, the appeal is more than offset by the difficulties involved in working with such a piece of nature. For Ghost, fourteen years later in 1994, construction involving an oak knee was preferred and would be repeated in 2001 and 2003, when Beaton's built two other A Cats: namely, Raven and Lightning.

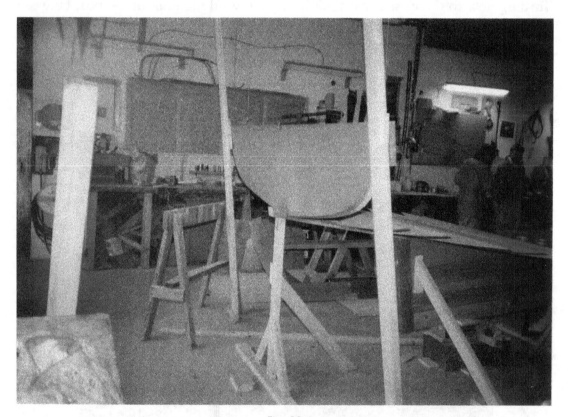

Fig. 18

Fig. 19

One component part remains to complete the core structure. It is the transom (figs. 18 and 19), which finds its place at the very end of the keel and serves to close off the end of the boat when it is afloat. It is made from a single piece of Central American mahogany. This wood is valued for its appearance and will in time become the bearer of the name "Ghost".

The positions of the several parts should be clear. What needs to be explained is how the parts are joined together.

1) In regard to the centerboard well, securing the headledges in place is relatively simple. The forward headledge is made to pass between bedlogs and into the keel. That provides a kind of anchor, which is strengthened by drilling holes through the bedlog on one side, through the headledge and out the bedlog on the other side. There bolts are inserted. The aft headledge is made to pass between bedlogs, through the keel and into the deadwood. Again bolts are inserted through the bedlogs.

2) Affixing the well to the bottom of the boat is more challenging. In the middle of the boat, it involves drilling vertical holes for bolts that pass though the bedlogs, then through the keel and finally into the deadwood. The bolts are long and their holes are drilled at different angles, in order that the bolts will not run parallel to each other. That adds strength to the join.

3) Still longer are the bolts used to secure the deadwood in the rear of the boat, for there the deadwood is quite deep. These bolts have to be specially made, in order that they can pass through the keel and reach counter-sunk holes within the deadwood. There bolt heads are firmly attached. When all these joins have been made, we might say that the keel is tightly sandwiched between bedlogs and deadwood.

4) The maststep must be attached to the bedlogs behind and to the stem in front. In Sweisguth's design the mast step is represented as overlapping the bedlogs (ch. II.2 fig.9). In building Ghost, preference was given to a tapered insert (male-female), which was secured by bronze bolts. The join forward to the stem involved notching and an overlapping knee (see fig. 17): one that is so positioned that it can be bolted not only to the stem but also to the bedlogs and the keel.

5) Finally, the transom was joined to the keel by cutting a small rectangular hole in the center bottom of the transom. There an end piece of the keel, cut to size, is inserted and attached with vertical screws (fig. 18). In addition, the interior face of the transom is attached to the keel by means of a vertical oak knee that runs along the keel and then extends upward to the top of the transom (fig. 19). The perimeter pieces of wood screwed to the interior face are known as doubling pieces and will be important later during planking. They will be used to accept the screws at the aft end of each hull plank. That eliminates the need to screw into the end grain of the transom, which is not good at holding the threads of a fastener.

The above remarks have explained the joining of parts in terms of position, interlocking connections and fasteners (bolts and screws). Not to be overlooked is the use of a sealant or epoxy glue, which is spread on the many contacting surfaces for additional strength and to prevent the intrusion of water, which over time can cause wood to become soft and in winter weather might cause a joint to loosen through expansion due to icing.

3) Framing and Planking the Hull

Before taking up the subject of framing and planking, it may be emphasized that the assembling of parts discussed in the preceding section has involved not only joining the parts but also joining them in such a way as to create an upright structure, which is lifted off the floor of the woodshop. That is already clear in several photos, which show supports attached to the floor: fig. 15 of the deadwood and figs. 18 and 19 of the transom. The height and position of each support is determined by measurements taken from the lofted lines. That includes aligning each support with designated marks along the bottom face of the keel. Not only are the supports plumbed to ensure that they are rising vertically from the floor, but also each is braced to prevent movement. With the same end in view, braces are attached to the ceiling from the transom and the stem (figs. 18 and 20). That can be tedious, but exact measurement is demanded, if a boat is to attain its proper shape. Long ago Aristotle had it right, when he wrote, "The beginning is more than half the whole."

Fig. 20

Framing begins with solid oak floor frames. Each of these frames has a straight, transverse horizontal line on the top edge. The bottoms differ in shape and bevel, being copied from a pattern made after the hull lines are lofted, i.e., after the lines are reproduced to full size. The frames well forward and aft in the boat are each one piece with one side a mirror image of the other side (figs. 20 and 21). These frames are fastened horizontally to the vertical bedlogs with either bolts or lag screws.

Fig. 21

The rest of the floor frames—those located in the middle of the boat along the side of the centerboard well and for some distance fore and aft of the well—are also mirror images on each side, but they are made as separate pieces. These frames are attached to the bedlogs with sections of bronze angles and horizontal bolts (see fig. 21 on the preceding page).

Fig. 22

Once the floor frames are in place and before planking begins, it is time for large building forms or molds to be set on top of the keel (fig. 22). They are made of multiple pieces of 1 ½ inch thick construction grade fir. The pieces are joined together with screws, in order that they can be removed easily from inside the hull after planking has been completed. The molds take their shape from the hull's lofted lines and are clamped in a vertical position at 90 degrees to the centerline. Being arranged in pairs, they represent a cross section of the hull at a designated point on the keel. There they are attached temporarily with angle brackets and to each other with planks of wood running across the boat. In addition, both sides of each pair are attached vertically to framework on the ceiling. That further protects the molds against unwanted movement. Indeed, since the molds determine the shape of the hull, great care must be taken not only to shape and position the molds correctly but also to secure them in place.

Once these several steps have been completed, it is time to introduce permanent stringers and temporary ribbands, both port and starboard (fig. 23). Most often professional boat builders refer to the permanent stringers as "clamps". Hence, in a technical manual "clamps" is to be preferred, but in the present book "stringers" will be preferred, in order that the lay reader not confuse the permanent clamps under consideration with metal clamps, which are temporary and used throughout the building process.

The permanent stringers are wooden planks that run the length of the hull. In the case of Ghost, Sitka spruce was used. Since finding a single plank of suitable quality and sufficient length is difficult, permanent stringers are often made of two planks joined together by scarfing (see below ch. II.5.2 with fig. 56), and so it is with Ghost.

The permanent stringers are of two kinds: There are sheer stringers, which find their place opposite the sheer plank or strake just below deck level. In that position, they are able to support the deck beams, which will be put in place once the hull is planked. There are also bilge stringers, which are found further down, more or less level with the waterline, when the boat is afloat (see below this section fig. 34). The aft end of each stringer is fastened to the interior face of the transom with an oak knee that is bolted in place (regarding the bilge and sheer stringers, see below ch. II.3.4 with figs. 39 and 40).

Like the permanent stringers, the temporary ribbands are wooden and run the length of the hull. They are 1½ inch square strips, made of construction grade fir and attached to the outside of the molds. When all the ribbands are in place, they will number approximately eight or nine on each side and will be spaced 3 to 4 inches apart.

Both the ribbands and stringers act as forms, around which the ribs will be bent (figs. 23 and 24). When possible, ribs are made from freshly cut white oak that has been

Fig. 23

Fig. 24

obtained from a local mill and has not had time to dry out. The specification "white" oak is important, because white oak is a stringy wood. In contrast to red oak, which is not stringy and which splits cleanly, white oak is so composed that it splits neither easily nor cleanly. That is a negative for the timber man who is splitting wood with a wedge, but for the boat builder it is a positive, in that white oak due to its natural composition does not split easily when bent. That makes it an ideal wood for making ribs that must be bent in order to accept curved planks, i.e., the planks that are to become the sides of an A Cat.

In the case of Ghost, each rib was sided 1 inch by 1¼ inch and cut to a length that is long enough to extend from the keel to several inches above the deck line of the hull. The ribs were then placed in the steam box in lots of 8-10 and allowed to absorb enough steam and heat to become pliant (see ch. II.1). While still very hot, the ribs were positioned against the side of the keel and next to a floor frame. The butt ends of the ribs were clamped in place and the ribs were slowly bent up against the outside surfaces of the ribbands and stringers. Several clamps were used to keep each rib tight against these bands in order that the proper hull shape might be achieved.

Fig. 25

In fig. 25 we see the rear of Ghost: port side and transom. Now the ribs are in place along the entire port side and presumably along the starboard side as well. Temporary vertical side posts and a center post are still in place to support the transom. Notice should be taken of the four ribbands, which appear under and behind the transom on each side of the keel. Above these ribbands, the heated moist ribs were slid into place against the keel. As the ribs were bent upward, the ribbands resisted the tendency of the ribs to push downward away from the keel.

After the ribs had cooled and their shape had set, they were fastened to the adjacent floor frames with horizontal bolts and riveted to each stringer.

Fig. 26

Once all the ribs had been fastened in place, they were subjected to final fairing, in order that when planking begins, the ribs will receive the planks evenly against a smooth surface. In fig. 26, Paul Smith is shown fairing the outer faces of steam bent ribs on the forward starboard side of the hull. He is using a handheld plane, which is the mark of a master craftsman. Plywood panels standing in the background act as a heat shield to prevent the nearby woodstove from overheating the hull of Ghost.

Fig. 27

The planking process begins with the top plank, which is known as the "sheer-strake". Like the transom, it is made of mahogany for strength (fig 27). Later the edge of the deck, the rubrail and the toe rail are all fastened to the sheerstrake. Hence, the importance of selecting a wood that brings strength to the topsides at their highest point, both port and starboard. Much the same is true of the garboard plank, which is next to the keel. It too is made of mahogany for strength.

The rest of the hull will be planked with Atlantic white cedar, which is rot resistant, bends easily and is lighter than mahogany. Given the importance of weight in regard to speed—lighter is faster—using cedar is all but mandatory.

In the photo, all of the construction molds are still in place with wood braces from each unit extending on an angle vertically to the woodshop ceiling. The upper ends of the braces are bolted to a special framework attached to the ceiling joists. The temporary horizontal stringers behind the ribs, i.e. the ribbands, will be removed after the planking is complete.

The person at work in the rear of the photo, i.e., at the bow of Ghost is Tom Beaton.

Fig. 28

In fig. 28, the planking continues. White cedar is used for the remainder of the hull. The boat is planked from the shear down and the keel up. The final plank is that at the turn of the bilge, i.e., the middle of the boat.

Underneath the boat is Paul. He is using an electric screwdriver to fasten planks to floor frames on the port side. His awkward position is made more comfortable by a custom made seat with backrest. Within the woodshop the seat was affectionately referred to as "lazy Russ"—a good natured and well received poke at Russ Manheimer.

Fig. 29

On the preceding page in fig. 29, the port side is completely planked. Paul is seated and smiling. The starboard side is almost completely planked. Space remains in the middle of the starboard side for a single plank, which is referred to as the shutter plank. It closes up the side, much as a common window shutter closes up the side of a house. Once the starboard shutter plank is in place, it will be time to remove the braces that rise to the ceiling; also the molds within the hull, to which the braces are attached.

Fig. 30

In fig. 30, the planking is complete. Paul's backrest is still under the boat but unoccupied. The wooden supports seen underneath the boat and running the length of the keel are still in place, but the wooden braces rising to the ceiling are gone. New are the metal tripods or "jackstands" capped with a padded block of wood. Their legs stand on the floor of the woodshop, while an adjustable rod lifts the padded block upward to meet the recently planked sides. That offers support, which will steady the boat as work inside the hull begins to take place.

The braces extending to the ceiling, the molds and ribbands have also been removed from the hull, but there is still work to be done. The planks need to be planed off and caulked, and the rivet/screw holes need to be filled.

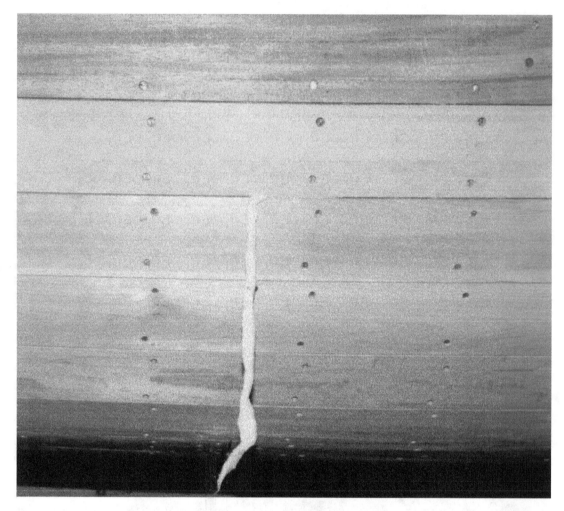

Fig. 31

Fig. 31 photo shows caulking cotton hanging from a seam of the hull into which it has been inserted. The photo may have been staged, but the practice was real and important. The planks of an A Cat's hull fit tightly on their inside faces but less so on the outside. Accordingly a small v-shaped opening is created in each seam on the outside of the planking. A twisted strand of soft untreated cotton is lightly driven into the seam with a caulking iron and wooden mallet. Prior to final sanding each seam opening is filled with a synthetic rubber compound that acts as a final seal against leakage.

Fig. 32

Mark Dawson is shown here driving wooden pegs into fastener holes on the port side. At the moment, he is working on the garboard plank. The plywood in the background is a heat shield against the woodstove. Cf. fig. 26 above.

Fig. 33

Moveable metal jackstands have been put in place to help support the hull (fig. 33). Especially clear is the boat's stem, i.e., the curved timber at the very front of boat, which is joined to the keel below and to which the side planks are joined on both sides. It is made of oak for strength and has been faired, so that the side planks join smoothly to the stem.

Most of the holes into which rivets/screws were driven have been filed with wooden pegs. The stem is exceptional in that four holes for fastening bolts are yet to be filled. One is round and three are square. Most likely the square holes were cut with a chisel, because no drill large enough was available at the time.

Fig. 34

Here we have the hull with all planks in place, both port and starboard (fig. 34). We are looking at the interior with all molds and construction forms removed. One can see the ribs to which the planks are peened. The athwart timbers (side to side bracing) are temporary. They keep the boat from spreading until the deck beams are installed. Visible on the sides are the longitudinal bilge and sheer stringers. And visible in the bottom of the boat are the floor frames, which will support a temporary floor while the deck beams are installed and the deck itself is laid. Also visible in the bottom is the beginning of the centerboard well: bedlogs, on which the sides of the well will rise, and headledges, which will become the ends of the fully constructed well. The opening through which the board will pass is eight feet ten inches long. That may seem excessively long for a 28-foot boat, but the A Cat is designed for a long board. See below ch. II.6.1.

4) Preparing for the Deck

Fig. 35

Work on the deck has begun with framing (fig. 35). On the sides and in the front of the boat (also in the rear; not shown in this photo), beams to carry the deck are in place. They have secured the shape of the hull, so that the athwart timbers have been removed. The open space seen in the photo will not all be open once the cabin has been constructed.

The "carlings" or "carlins", i.e., the curved longitudinal timbers that form the shape of the inner edge of the deck, have been fit and fastened in place. Note the temporary vertical braces supporting the middle of each carling

The forward main beam is in place. It runs perpendicular to the centerline of the boat. The semi-circular framework that will determine the shape of the front of the cabin has yet to be installed immediately aft of the main beam (see figs. 36 and 37). The beams forward in the boat show a gentle slope that will characterize the deck at this point.

Temporary flooring is also in place, so that further work on the beams and on the deck proper can proceed without fear of breaking an ankle or otherwise hurting oneself.

Fig. 36

All forward deck beams have now been fit and fastened (fig. 36). A semi-circular framework has been installed at the forward end of the deck opening. That provides the curved base for the forward lower edge of the steam bent mahogany cabin side.

In the photo, one sees the lower centerline cable that is stretched between the vertical bow brace and a center post aft. Not seen is a similar center cable still in position just below the shop ceiling. The higher cable is used for all centering measurements until the hull is completed. The lower cable is then installed at a height that is easier to access while working on the deck and the interior. A plumb line dropped from either cable will always indicate the exact centerline of the vessel from the stem to the transom.

Fig. 37

In fig. 37, the focus is on the deck beams at the forward end of the deck opening. The carling is seen to be notched and the deck beams fitted into the cavities. More important, we see that the semi-circular framework is not a single piece of wood. Rather, it is made of three pieces which are bolted to the carling and to the forward main deck beam. While the primary purpose of the semi-circular shape is to provide a curved surface to which the cabin sides can be affixed, it will also add strength at the point where the forward main beam and the decking terminate.

Fig. 38

Here again we see the forward beams with their gentle slope as well as the semi-circular framework that will determine the curve of the cabin (fig. 38). New is the blocking between beams and around the mast hole. In addition, we see horizontal lodging knees and the upper parts of vertical hanging knees. Also visible are two bronze straps that cross each other on top of the forward beams. They will further strengthen the hull against twisting when under sail. The deck proper will cover the straps. That is already called for by Sweisguth in his deck plan dated March 1923 (see ch. II.2 fig. 9), only Sweisguth prefers steel straps and not bronze as were used in building Ghost.

Fig. 39

Fig. 39 shows the rear of Ghost. In particular, we see that the aft starboard side of the deck is completely framed. Two L-shaped bolts that attach side deck beams to the carling are visible. In addition, it is clear that the transom is in place. It is secured not only by screws that can be seen in the photo but also by vertical oak knees. There is a thicker knee in the center of the transom and thinner knees toward the sides, of which one is visible in the photo. Once again we see a metal strap as called for by the Sweisguth plan of March 1923 (fig. 9).

Fig. 40

In fig. 40 we have the aft framing of the deck on the port side. Seen in the upper right is a horizontal quarter-knee that connects the transom to the aft end of the sheer plank and the sheer stringer/clamp, which can be seen below and between the deck beams. In addition, a one-piece rectangular gusset type timber forms a ridged support for the connection of the aft main beam and the aft end of the port carling. Its primary purpose is to strengthen the hull against twisting. The gusset also acts as an anchor point for the bronze strap that runs across the aft deck beams. As on the starboard side, so here the bronze strap is intended to strengthen the hull against twisting.

Sweisguth's March plan (fig. 9) is similar in that it shows a metal strap crossing the aft main beam and the end of the port carling at the same point. The plan differs in that it appears to call for horizontal knees rather than a one-piece rectangular gusset. The difference is real but comparatively minor, when one considers that Beaton's has followed Sweisguth in strengthening the hull against twisting at the aft end of the cockpit.

5) The Deck in Place

The first A Cat built by Beaton's, i.e. Wasp, had a deck made of cedar planks, which were ¾ inch thick, laid on top of beams and glued together for strength. Ghost's deck is different: it is made of 1/2 inch Okoume Marine Grade Plywood—a plantation grown African mahogany—which is light as well as strong, easily worked, and takes epoxy well. That is an improvement in that mahogany plywood creates a stiffer deck, which strengthens the hull. To be sure, Ghost's deck is not made out of a single sheet of plywood. But the sheets are fewer than in a deck made of boards, and in the case of Ghost the several sheets fit together tightly. They are scarfed (on scarfing, see ch. II.5.2 with fig. 56), glued together and fastened to the deck beam structure by screws. Below we have two photos. One is taken from the rear of Ghost and the other from the front. In both the deck has been laid, trimmed and faired to shape. That tells us that the photos were made after the Last Rivet Party, at which time a portion of the deck had not been laid and trimming had not begun. See ch. II.4 fig. 47.

Fig. 41

Here, in fig. 41, we are looking at Ghost from the rear. The bank of clamps on both sides of the deck represent a late stage in the decking, which began in the rear of the boat (see ch. II.4 fig. 47) and moved forward. Similarly the clamps on the centerboard well (on which see ch. II.7.1) tell us that the well has recently been under construction.

On both sides across from the centerboard well, we see the bottom of a vertical knee. On the left it is near a moveable lamp and on the right it is near a stray water bottle. The knee is attached to a rib and supports the deck above. On the other side of the rib, a wooden block is visible. It strengthens a joint where two planks of the hull come together. On both sides, below the knee and block, the longitudinal bilge stringer is seen.

Fig. 42

Now in fig. 42 we see Ghost from the front. The many individual blotches (also seen is fig. 41) are the result of filling depressions where screws have been sunk. As a filling an epoxy putty has been used and where necessary sanded smooth. The blotches that line up laterally tell us that the deck is attached to individual beams in multiple places.

Toward the bottom of the photo and in the middle, the mast hole is visible. In Sweisguth's design (ch. II.2 fig. 9), the location of the hole is the same, but there is a difference. Whereas Sweisguth's design exhibits a round hole anticipating a round mast at deck level, Ghost's mast hole is square, anticipating a square mast at deck level. The blotches around the mast hole cover depressions where the deck is attached to bracing underneath the deck. Through the hole, one can see two pieces of wood that have been glued together. These pieces, perhaps as many as four, are not only glued but also bolted together. The composite is called the mast partner. It strengthens the deck greatly against sideward pressures exerted by the mast in windy, stormy conditions.

The line of fill aft of the mast hole most likely marks a join between two sheets of plywood.

After the coaming is in place, the deck will be covered with xynole. See ch. II.5.3 with figs. 60 and 61.

4. The Last Rivet

When the framing of Ghost's bottom and topsides had been completed and the planking of the same was approaching completion, it was almost Christmas time. One of the builders—perhaps it was Russ Manheimer—suggested that it would be fun to hold a "last rivet party." Bill Fortenbaugh had to ask what such a party might be and was told that there was a tradition in shipbuilding that called for celebrating the completion of riveting the hull together. Much as the construction of a metal bridge or high-rise building involves a moment in which the last rivet is put in place, so with a boat there is a moment when the last plank is peened to the frame. And the rivet used in peening that plank is celebrated as the last rivet. Bill was impressed by the explanation, and the idea of holding a party so appealed to him, that a celebration was planned for the Sunday before Christmas.

On the designated Sunday, a crowd gathered in the woodshop at Beaton's not only to witness the final act of peening but also to partake of Old Overholt, a real rye whisky that has its roots in Pennsylvania and was still consumed by a handful of folk who hailed from Philadelphia. As a chaser or simply to be consumed on its own, Rheingold beer was also made available.

Fig. 43

Once the crowd had become jolly, Santa Claus appeared and offered a toast—rye whisky, of course—to young and old alike (fig. 43). Several bottles of Old Overholt can be seen on the table behind Santa as well as a quart bottle of Rheingold beer. Santa is seen raising his glass in salute to Ghost and to all the friends of Ghost who have assembled in the woodshop. Behind and to the right of Santa is Anne Edwards, wife of Rod, who was a member of Ghost's original crew. The youngster in the foreground is Alex Vienckowski, son of Ed and Bev (fig. 45 and ch. VIII.1 with fig. 151). He seems to be fascinated by Santa. Late in the summer of 1994, he would be in the cabin when Ghost tipped over during a blow. Not a good place to have been: a lesson was learned (ch. VI.2 end).

After Santa's words of welcome, Kearney Kuhlthau climbed up and into Ghost (fig. 44), in order to lead the singing of the Rheingold song.

Fig. 44

My beer is Rheingold
the dry beer.
Think of Rheingold whenever
you buy beer.
It's not bitter, not sweet;
it's the extra dry treat.
Won't you try extra dry
Rheingold beer?

Kearney was a long time friend of the Fortenbaughs and a sailor as well. Indeed he was a member of the Yacht Club at Green Pond, north and west of Barnegat Bay, where he raced Sunfish. He was also a member of a barbershop quartet and pleased to lead the singing of the Rheingold Song, not only at the Last Rivet Party, but also at the Launching of Ghost (ch. V.2).

There never was any doubt that Ghost would be closely identified with Rheingold beer. Not only was Rheingold hugely popular among sailors on Barnegat Bay, but also Bill had worked on the Rheingold delivery truck two summers while in college. He was the grunt for the driver, George Layton. At every stop, Bill was treated along with George to a shot of whiskey and a Rheingold chaser. Little work was accomplished after lunch.

The Rheingold song was already well known to sailors on the Bay, but it would become even more popular, when it was adopted by the crew of Ghost as their fight song. Indeed, over the years four Rheingold flags—battle flags—would be made and flown from Ghost's mast when the boat was at anchor or under tow. Three of the four flags were, as it were, traditional. They imitated the label that distinguished a bottle of Rheingold from less tasty brands.

In fig. 45, we see Bill and Ed Vienckowski holding up one of the traditional flags. The photo was taken at Bill's 80th birthday party, but the flag dates back to 1994, the year Ghost was launched. It is especially appropriate that Ed is shown holding the flag with Bill, for he was a member of the original crew and central to Ghost's success on the racecourse (see below, in fig. 49 and ch. VI.1-2).

A fourth flag would be donated by Dan Crabbe when he came aboard during Ghost's seventh season. It cleverly identified Ghost with Rheingold beer (ch. VI.3 fig 141).

Fig. 45

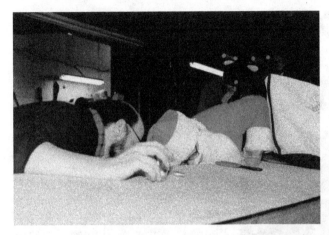

Fig. 46

Fig. 47

After the singing of the Rheingold song, Russ took over the program and called on Santa to receive instructions in peening the last rivet. Santa obliged and was seen looking under the deck as Russ pointed to the spot where the rivet would be located. In fig.46, Russ is holding a glass that appears to be empty. Santa's glass still holds some whisky, but only because Santa has enjoyed several refills. The result is obvious in the photo that follows.

To no one's surprise, Santa suffered a tumble (fig. 47): Having lost his balance, he is on his back in the bottom of the boat behind the centerboard well. Only his boots and part of one leg are visible. Russ is amused as are the spectators outside the boat. The photographer is Dick Speck, who is responsible for many of photographs reproduced in this book.

In the lower left corner, one sees that the deck is unfinished. The cross beams are in place but they await the plywood, which will be affixed to the beams. That tells us that the deck was put together out of several pieces of plywood and that the Last Rivet Party was held before the decking was complete. That is not a contradiction, for the plywood deck was not secured with rivets. To be sure, rivets would be used elsewhere, e.g., in attaching a gudgeon to the bottom of the keel in order to support the rudder (see below ch. II.6.2 fig. 72), but only a captious quibbler would see that as a contradiction.

Noticeable also is the centerboard well, which was lacking sides when work on the deck began (see ch. II.3.3 fig. 34). In the present photo, we see that sides have been added during work on the deck.

Russ wisely gave up on Santa and turned to Sheldon Pisani, who was known to be reliable and steady on her feet. Russ suggested that she take a position outside the boat on the starboard side. There she has in her hands a tool that is affectionately

Fig. 48

known as a "Bucking Dolly". The smile on Sheldon's face suggests that she knows full well what some of the spectators are thinking. But she cares little. Her primary concern is a single copper rivet that needs to be secured in place. Otherwise the gathering will fail to be the Last Rivet Party.

Sheldon held the Dolly in place, while Russ hammered what had been a copper nail into a secure rivet. When that had been accomplished, some smart-mouth called aloud, asking when the "golden" rivet would be peened. Two persons laughed. They had understood, but others were either ignorant or decorous and remained silent. Either way, Sheldon was not embarrassed, and the last rivet was in place.

To name all the persons who came to witness the last rivet being peened would be tedious—it would smack of padding—but three may be singled for special mention. One is Jane Carpenter Post who came in a Christmas costume that added twenty years to her appearance. She said that she was impersonating Mrs. Santa Claus. Jane learned to sail in Mantoloking—the Carpenters were a Manto family—but dared to marry Bob Post, a Bay Header. Six months after the Last Rivet Party, Bob would commemorate Ghost's first race in song (ch. VI.1).

A second person is Ed Vienckowski (already mentioned above). In fig. 49, he is pictured with his arm around Jane. The presence of Ed at the party was of special importance, for early during the event Bill asked him to come on Ghost and trim the sail while calling tactics. Ed sensed a winner and agreed. The timing was serendipitous, for later during the party Chris

Fig. 49

Chadwick asked Ed to come on board Mary Ann. Ed declined, having committed to Bill. It is hard not to remember the good fortune Bill had in asking Tom Beaton to build an A Cat only a week or two before Peter Kellogg put the same request to Tom (ch. I.2).

The third person is Roy Wilkins. He might be called Mr. A Cat, for his impressive stature exhibits the power of an A Cat and his enthusiasm resembles that of the sailors who compete within the class. Not surprisingly Roy would be present and speak at the launching of Ghost (ch. V.2), but at the last rivet gathering he is memorable for a prescient moment. Engaging Bill in conversation, he expressed foreboding, commenting that Bill's two sons, Michael and Peter, were excellent sailors. Apparently he drew a backward looking inference: if the children, then the father. The conclusion would be proven true, but the premise was only half the story. One needs to add that the children's involvement in sailing, especially E Scow racing, had made Bill aware of the talented younger sailors on Barnegat Bay. In particular, it familiarized him with Ed Vienckowski, who earlier during the party had agreed to come aboard Ghost. Moreover, Ed would be accompanied by his wife Bev Carr (see ch. VIII.1 fig. 151), who had grown up sailing at the Bay Head Yacht Club, where the Carr family were members. Without such talent, Ghost might well have been an also-ran.

5. Cabin, Coaming, and Xynole

The heading to this section mentions three items, but the subsequent discussion is divided into four subsections. 1) Here the focus is on the sides of the cabin: its bending and attachment to the inner rim of the deck. After that the focus shifts to 2) coaming, then to 3) covering the deck and finally to 4) completing the cabin. Xynole, an open-weave polyester laminating fabric, might have been discussed in a special subsection, thereby emphasizing its importance in the construction of Ghost, but because it is important to both the deck and to the cabin, in particular its roof, it will be discussed within two subsections: 3) and 4). In addition, the construction of Ghost's cabin doors might have been discussed in subsection 4), for work on the entry into the cabin anticipates the hanging of doors. Nevertheless the doors not only have a charm all their own but also can be viewed as an extra item, for they are being omitted in younger boats. For discussion of the cabin doors, see ch. II.7

1) Cabin Sides and Bending Jig

Once the plywood deck was in place, trimmed and holes filed, it was time for constructing the cabin sides. They would be made from a single plank of mahogany which would be bent and affixed forward to the inner rim of the deck. In smaller boats like the fifteen foot Sneakbox, such a bent plank is primarily a shield against water entering the cockpit when waves are breaking on the bow. It functions as a splash rail or board. In an A Cat, the plank has not lost that function, but it is also fundamental to the cabin. It becomes the curved enclosure that supports the roof of the cabin. Moreover, enhanced by several coats of varnish, it provides a handsome contrast when viewed against the color of the deck as well as against the topsides—especially, the dark green sides of Ghost when seen at a distance on the brownish water that is characteristic of Barnegat Bay.

Fig. 50

In preparation for putting the cabin sides in place, a frame—in the woodshop it is called a "bending jig"—has been constructed (fig. 50). It is a temporary vertical framework that has been installed within the boat forward of the centerboard well. It will be used for bending the sides of the cabin. That is, it will be used for forming the semi-circular front of the cabin. In the photo, the jig is seen from outside the boat on the port side.

Fig. 51

In fig. 51 the jig is seen from inside the boat. The structure of the bending jig is ready for bending a twenty foot mahogany plank. The plank will first be subjected to hot steam (on the boiler and the steam box, see ch. II. 1), after which it will be bent and attached to the jig in a position above the deck. It will remain there until it cools. The plank will then be loosened and slowly slid down into its final position, where it becomes the sides and front wall of Ghost's cabin.

The number of clamps arranged together on top of the centerboard well is impressive. They will be used first to hold the heated plank to the rig and second to hold the plank, once it has cooled and been slid down into its final position.

Fig. 52

In fig. 52 steaming has occurred, so that the mahogany plank pictured here is ready to be bent. In the photo it has been removed from the steam box and centered on the bending jig. Tom is seen centering the plank before it is bent. He has a clamp in one hand and a block of wood in the other. On the left, Russ is holding one end of the plank; someone else is doing the same on the other side of the boat.

The ends of the plank, now quite pliable, will be slowly forced against the bending jig and clamped until the entire plank is held tightly against the uprights of the jig. The thin block of wood held by Tom (fig. 52) is being clamped to the center of the upper half of the plank, where it will act as a compression strip that resists splitting on the outside face of the plank. The block will be removed after the plank has cooled.

Fig. 53

Fig. 54

Fig. 55

In fig. 53 the mahogany plank has been successfully bent and clamped to the bending jig. The actual bending is a nerve-wracking task that requires not a few hands to bend and to clamp the plank around the jig. In the photo, we see Paul and Tom working together outside the jig. Inside are Mark Dawson and Russ. Spectators were discouraged from being in attendance. The exception was Dick "RT" Speck, who was permitted to photograph the event.

Here in fig. 54 we have the bent mahogany plank moved down to its final position against the inside edge of the deck. The entire bending jig has been removed. The plank is securely clamped and partially fastened in place with screws. More will be added.

A different view (fig. 55) from the starboard side of Ghost shows the side and front of the cabin fastened in place but not trimmed to its final height from the deck.

One sees that the plywood deck is still unfinished: it has not received a xynole covering. One wonders whether it might have been better (easier, more effective) to cover the deck before attaching the cabin (and the coaming to the rear as well). But whatever the rationale, work on the cabin took precedence.

2) Coaming

Fig. 56

Enclosing the cabin area is followed by enclosing the cockpit area immediately aft of the cabin. Unlike the cabin, the cockpit will not be covered, but it will be enclosed by mahogany planks that descend in height and surround the cockpit port and starboard (but not across the rear). Although these planks are effectively an extension of the cabin sides, in sailing parlance they are normally referred to as "coaming". Joining the coaming to the cabin sides is accomplished by "scarfing": a method of joining boards not by placing butt-end against butt-end but by tapering, i.e., gradually diminishing the thickness of two boards, so that they will overlap in an all but seamless manner (fig. 56). The taper is usually cut at a ratio of twelve inches in length for every inch of thickness. The cabin sides and the coaming are ¾ inch thick, so that the length of the scarf, the overlap, is nine inches. That creates a join with considerable surface. When glued together and fastened to the side of the cockpit, the boards do not come apart.

The scarf joints on Ghost are special in that the scarf on each board is cut back slightly to form a straight line that will fit into a matching notch at the base of each scarf. That is referred to as a "nib scarf".

Figs. 57 and 58 on the next page show the joining of the cabin side and the coaming. Fig. 57 shows the join from within on the starboard side. Fig. 58 shows the join from the outside. The boards have been glued and are being held together by clamps. The descent of the coaming aft of the cabin is visible as is the extension of the coaming over the rear deck.

Fig. 57

Fig. 58

Fig. 59

Now in fig. 59 the glue has dried and Russ has removed the clamps and the up-right boards that had been used to hold the two pieces of mahogany tightly together. He is preparing to trim and sand the area.

3) Covering the Deck

Fig. 60

Fig. 61

In figs. 60 and 61, the cabin sides and coaming have already been trimmed to their final height and shape. Now the plywood deck is covered with xynole, a synthetic material quite different from the traditional canvas, which Beaton's used when building Wasp (ch. I.1). That was 1980. Some fourteen years later, 1994, Beaton's has changed to a polyester material. In the photos, the material has been stretched and smoothed on the plywood, after which it was coated with an epoxy resin that has penetrated the cloth and glued it to the surface of the plywood deck. The excess cloth seen on the edges of the deck will be trimmed to a smooth finish.

When set in epoxy, xynole adds strength to the deck and does not tear in the way that canvas does. It is, as it were, impact and abrasion resistant. In addition, it provides a non-skid surface until several coats of paint make it slippery. That is a problem hardly unique to xynole. A non-skid paint may be the easiest and best remedy.

Noteworthy in fig. 60 is the transparency of the cloth. An epoxy coating has already been applied, but it allows the surface below the cloth to be visible. Hence one sees the filling that covers the several joints in the plywood deck.

Also noteworthy is the white material between the cabin sides and the deck. It is a synthetic rubber caulking material, which seals the join and prevents water from entering. Were that allowed to happen, rotting might occur in the wooden structure.

In fig. 61, one sees that the aft ends of the coaming have not been fastened down to the deck. That has made it possible to run the xynole under the coaming on the rear deck without cutting the material. Once epoxy has been applied and dried, the ends of the coaming will be fastened down.

At this stage the topsides of Ghost and the bottom including the deadwood have not been painted.

4) The Cabin Completed

Fig. 62

Once the deck of Ghost was covered and sealed, it was time to return to the cabin, whose sides had been put in place before being joined to the coaming, which ran aft along the sides of the open cockpit. The cabin needed a roof, and that required beams, which extended from side to side and were slightly curved, thereby creating a roof that sheds water easily. Such beams are either cut to the required curve or are laminated wood strips that are glued and clamped on a frame of the proper shape.

Fig. 62 shows Tom busy framing the cabin top, in preparation for laying Okoume plywood atop the frames.

Fig. 63

Fig. 63 shows the roof in place. The rear edge is visible in that it overhangs the entry into the cabin. One can see into the cabin between the two side panels, left and right. They are made of mahogany plywood and define the entry into the cabin. The roof beams are visible within the cabin. One also sees the large, curved stretch of mahogany that forms the front of the cabin. Further forward in the boat and low, three boards that cross from side to side are visible. A fourth is barely visible. They are shaped to join the ribs and are designed to strengthen the bow, where the foot of the mast will put increased pressure on the hull in heavy wind.

The centerboard well, which begins in the open cockpit, extends forward into the cabin, dividing it in two. This extension into the cockpit has some negative effects: it makes it more difficult to get water out of the bilge (if alone, one must change sides) and for sweethearts it functions like an old fashioned bundling board. But it also encourages dividing up stored equipment in a way that makes access easy, and it creates personal space, so that two fatigued crew members can rest below between races or during a tow without bothering each other (unless one snores).

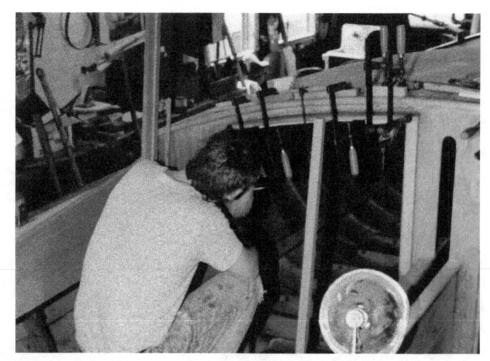

Fig. 64

Fig. 65

In fig. 63 (two pages earlier) the panels that form the entry into the cabin are bare: both the side pieces and the curved portion underneath the overhang of the cabin roof. Now in fig. 64 we see Mark Dawson adding to the port doorway, and in fig. 65 we see the results of his work, both port and starboard. On the sides and above both entryways, strips have been added. They make the entry into the cabin only slightly tighter, but that is not their purpose. They anticipate the doors, which will be hung, and will make it possible to close the doors without leaving space through which mosquitos and other pesky creatures can enter the cabin. In addition, mahogany drip caps have been attached above both entryways.

In both photos, but especially in fig. 65, we can see that the temporary flooring within the cabin has been removed. It will soon be replaced by a permanent floor.

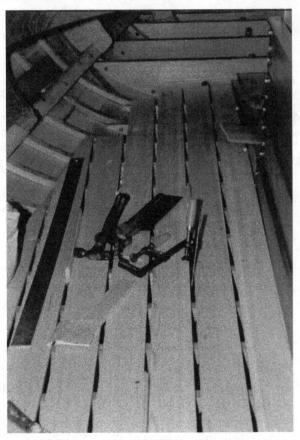

Fig. 66

Fig. 66 shows the port side cabin "sole", i.e., the permanent floor, which is being installed. The planks are three-quarters of an inch thick and made of white cedar. Since a light boat is a fast boat, weight was a consideration in choosing the kind and thickness of the planks. That was true in 1994 when Ghost was built, but later when the A Cat class voted to impose a minimum weight on boats competing in class sponsored races, lighter boats were required to add lead in specified places. That stimulated clever minds: it encouraged the use of heavy planks in the cabin area and the addition of heavy blocks of wood under the flooring in the open cockpit. But additional weight well forward in the cabin area and in the rear of the cockpit was not desirable, and in general the time and cost involved in making changes to the existing flooring was not justified by a minimum gain—if any—in speed. Members of the class soon recognized that a better way to win was to get off the starting line first and to avoid tacking duels out on the course.

More important is the space left between the planks. In fig. 66, to the left and second plank in, one can see a board sticking up between two planks. See also the fourth plank at the foot of the photo. Using boards in this manner is an easy way to measure the distance between the planks. And the distance is intended to be sufficient for air to circulate between the bottom of the hull, the bilge, and the floor, thereby keeping the flooring drier and lighter than it would be in the absence of space between the several planks.

Fig. 67

Fig. 67 provides a clear picture of the entry into the cabin and of the cabin itself. Mark's additions to the panels around the entry are easy to see and so are the planks within the cabin. When exactly the photo was taken is not easy to pin down, but we can say that painting the ceiling of the cabin white did not occur immediately after the flooring was put down. For Tom had to persuade Bill that visibility within the cabin was more important than additional varnish. Certainly Ghost was not hurting for lack of varnish: the panels and trim to the entry are shining with varnish. Be that as it may, the interior of the cabin would also benefit from other sources of light. On each side of the cabin a window would be installed. That would let light in, and since the windows could be opened, they would also contribute to ventilation.

Interestingly, Sweisguth's 1923 drawings for Tamwock, both March and November (ch. II.2 figs. 9 and 10) show two windows, not one, for each side of the boat. (*Re vera*, Sweisguth's drawings show the starboard side of Tamwock, but extrapolating to both sides is reasonable.) Whether Sweisguth was committed to pairs of windows cannot be determined. His drawings may be merely suggestive. What he will not have considered and what Ghost obtained was a cabin light powered by the battery that also powered a pump to clear the bilge after rain and heavy seas.

For completeness' sake, it should be noticed that Sweisguth's March design (ch. II.2 fig. 9) calls for a sliding hatch on the starboard side of the cabin top. That too would let in light and increase ventilation, but it may have been more for the comfort of gentlemen sailors. The finer people of the 1920s would not have to stoop or crawl to go below. In any case, the cabin hatch appears in Sweisguth's March sail plan. Its absence in the November sail plan is unimportant (ch. IV.1 figs. 87 and 88). For the focus is on sails and spars: details concerning the cabin top are irrelevant. Moreover, since Mary Ann, Bat, Spy and Lotus all had a sliding cabin hatch, it would be wild speculation to think that Sweisguth seriously considered omitting a sliding hatch. And when Beaton's built Wasp in 1980 they followed Sweisguth's hull design and made a hatch for Wasp. Ghost is another story. There Beaton's did omit the hatch and for good reason. A sliding hatch would be an additional expense and would contribute nothing to winning races. Indeed, by adding weight and windage, it might be considered a detriment.

What may astonish is the floor to the cockpit, which is visible at the bottom of fig. 67. Here no special effort has been made to leave space between each plank. Indeed, it was deemed safer not to have gaps between the planks: no stumbles or lost fittings. In the photo at the bottom toward the left, one does see a single crack and a slightly larger gap. That is intentional, but the primary purpose was not ventilation. Rather the plank in question is intended to be removable, so that one can get at the bilge, either to remove water (pumping or sponging) or to rescue something that has made its way into the bilge. Fair enough, but it was still possible to give the bilge a modest airing by taking up the removable plank when at dock or under tow. Most often it was stored under a bench in the cockpit.

Just as the mahogany plywood deck was covered with xynole, a polyester cloth, and then sealed with epoxy, so too the plywood cabin top—also Okoume mahogany—would be protected with xynole and epoxy. In figs. 68 and 69, xynole has already been stretched out on the cabin top. Now William Gorman, who was primarily a mechanic but also worked with fiberglass at Beaton's, is seen in the process of saturating the material with epoxy resin. Willie, as he was known around the yard, is wearing a

breathing mask to protect himself against the toxic fumes given off by the resin. He is using both a brush and a roller. The latter makes it possible to saturate large areas more quickly. The former allows greater control when needed.

Paper has been applied to the cabin sides to mask the surface against possible drips of epoxy.

Fig. 68   Fig. 69

6. Centerboard, Rudder and Tiller

There are several parts of an A Cat, which are essential to the boat but may be viewed as distinct from the hull in that they can be made separately from the hull—before, after and during the construction of the hull—and can be removed from the hull for repair and replacement without disturbing the hull. They are the spars, i.e., the mast and boom, which will be the subject of Chapter V, and the centerboard, rudder and tiller, which may viewed in Sweisguth's plans (see ch. II.2) and which will be discussed here in three subsections.

1) The Centerboard

As the name indicates the centerboard finds its position in the middle of the hull. Its primary purpose is to keep the boat sailing forward by preventing slippage sideways. In the case of Ghost the board is made of mahogany, but not a single piece. Rather two sheets of sapele plywood are joined together with epoxy glue In addition, lead is added to the board in order to keep it submerged when it is lowered into the water. After shaping, the surfaces of the centerboard are covered with two layers of fiberglass cloth set in epoxy resin. That creates a strong board, which resists bending under pressure.

The centerboard is encased within what is often referred to as a "well". The metaphor is easily understood. Like a farmer's dug well, which is a vertical opening that leads downward to water, so the sailor's well is a vertical shaft that leads downward to water, i.e., the water on which a boat floats and sails. Instead of lowering a bucket to draw water as a farmer might do, the sailor lowers the centerboard, which offers resistance when wind or tide wants to push the boat off course.

The preceding is not meant to deny that the centerboard well is also referred to as a "trunk", which is not an inappropriate label. One might think of a container for luggage: e.g., the large containers formerly used by elegant people when traveling at sea. So too the centerboard trunk is a container that looms large within an A Cat: it extends backward into the cockpit and forward into the cabin. Only its contents are not the luggage of a tourist but rather the centerboard, which is essential to an A Cat.

In an A Cat the bottom of the centerboard well sits on the keel, into which an opening 1 3/4 inches wide and 8 feet 10 inches long has been cut (see above ch. II.3.3 end with fig. 34). The sides of the well begin with mahogany bedlogs, on top of which boards, also made of mahogany, are arranged horizontally. In Paul Smith's adaptation (fig. 70) of Sweisguth's March plan (fig. 9), the horizontal boards are three (on each side of the well). They are secured together and to the bedlogs below by vertical bronze drift rods set at different angles. These rods prevent the boards from separating. In addition, each board is attached to the headledges with bolts. When the well is finished, it will rise approximately 36 inches above the keel (the qualifier "approximately" takes account of the fact that the keel plank exhibits a gradual rise fore and aft; see Sweisguth's design ch. II.2 fig. 8).

The length of the opening, approaching nine feet, is striking and part of the architect's design. That may seem odd, for upper Barnegat Bay, where A Cats normally race (see ch. VI.2), is not especially deep—in many places only four feet deep—so that a centerboard measuring eight feet six inches in length will rarely be lowered to full depth. True, but being long and pivoting, the board need not be lowered fully to do its work.

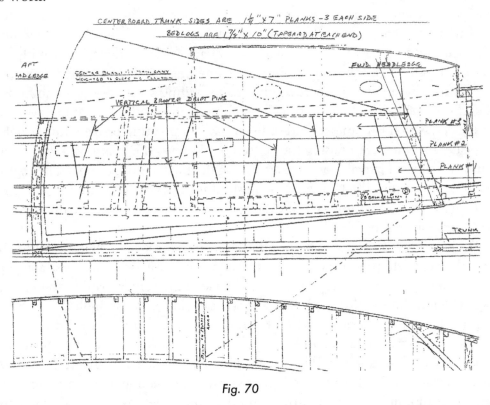

Fig. 70

Here it may be helpful to distinguish between a daggerboard and a pivoting board. The former is raised up and down, most often manually, and will be found in small boats like the Sail Fish that became popular in the 1950s. Oldsters will remember the Duck Boat as it used to be found on upper Barnegat Bay and is still found in Little Egg Harbor under the name "Sneakbox". Originally designed for a practical purpose, hunting waterfowl, the Duck Boat was only twelve feet long and had the simplest possible well: a straight shaft in which a daggerboard was moved up and down by hand. Sometime in the nineteen-fifties Phil Clark changed the design by introducing a pivoting centerboard: one that involves a bolt or rod down low and forward in the well, around which the board pivots. The change was an improvement that had precedent on Barnegat Bay. It was long a feature of the 15-foot Sneakbox or "Perrine" as the folk in Little Egg Harbor say. And, of course, the pivoting board was part of the earliest A Cats built in the 1920s.

Unlike a daggerboard, a pivoting board that is long exposes considerable area without being lowered to full depth. The exposed surface increases toward the rear of the board—think of a folding fan that is pinned at one end and opens at the other—so that the board, in combination with the deadwood and rudder, provides sufficient lateral resistance to prevent slippage sideways. And it does so in comparatively shallow water, where lowering the board further is not possible. But that is not all. Even in deep water where it is possible to sail with full board, one may choose not to sail upwind with full board. That violates the oft-repeated rule of thumb: sail upwind with full board, reach across the wind with less board and run downwind with as little board as possible. The problem here is that upwind in a breeze, the A Cat tends to have a strong weather helm. If the helmsman is sailing with full board, he finds himself fighting the helm. He is continually pulling the boat off, and that involves turning the rudder, which becomes a kind of brake. With a pivoting board weather helm can be greatly mitigated. For raising the centerboard moves the board backwards and that shifts the center of lateral resistance aft, giving the boat a more balanced helm. Indeed, speaking of "raising" the board can be misleading, for when the adjustment is minor, the board moves aft without significantly reducing the area of the board that is in the water preventing slippage.

When an A Cat is sailing before the wind in light air, the centerboard is hardly needed. Lateral slippage is rarely an issue, and the deadwood can resist any slippage that might arise during a slight change in course. If the centerboard is down, it creates drag, which is slow, so that the board is best raised, but never so high that it creates an opening at the bottom of the well. That too creates drag. There are, however, exceptions. In a heavy wind and a following sea, the board is lowered enough to achieve stability, i.e., to eliminate rocking or "wallowing" which is a greater detriment to speed than too much board. It is also lowered when sailing across a strong current: e.g., when running from one buoy to another takes the boat across a strong current created by a flooding or ebbing channel to the ocean.

2) The Rudder

Almost all sailboats have a rudder, which finds its place toward the rear of the boat. To be sure, some sailboats have two rudders like the E Scow, which needs a port and a starboard rudder, because it is sailed on its side, i.e., on a heel. And there is the windsurfer that has no rudder; it is controlled by adjusting the sail and shifting weight. But these boats are exceptional. The A Cat is ordinary/traditional in that it has a single rudder, which is placed well aft.

For a 28-foot boat, the size of an A Cat's rudder is comparatively large. Allowing for individual variation, we can say that it has a mean length of c. 4 feet 3 inches and a height that is c. 2 feet 3 inches in front and c. 2 feet 6 inches in the rear. A well-balanced racing boat like the E Scow, which also is 28 feet, has a much smaller rudder. The traditional rectangular rudder measures 12 inches deep and no more than 21 inches in length. The new spade rudder is 16 inches high and at its widest 10 inches fore and aft. But the A Cat is a very different boat, for which large is better than small. In heavy wind an A Cat can be hard to steer both upwind and downwind. Upwind, an A Cat is apt to have a strong weather helm, so that a large rudder helps the helmsman keep the boat on its proper course. To be sure, loosening the leech and removing draft from the sail (IV.2), or reefing the sail, adjusting the centerboard and having large bodies on the weather rail are the preferred ways to deal with a weather helm. But when the wind comes up quickly and when the wind approaches fifteen to twenty knots a large rudder can be quite helpful. And downwind with a following sea, the helmsman may have trouble steering, so that here too a large rudder is desirable. Indeed, during a jibe, when the helmsman wishes to begin the maneuver quickly and to turn back as soon as the sail begins to cross the center of the boat, a large rudder can make a difference (see ch. VI.1 penultimate paragraph).

In Sweisguth's hull plans, those of March and that of November (ch. II.2 figs. 9 and 10), the rudder proper, i.e., the rudderblade is attached to a post or shaft that extends above the rear deck (affectionately known as the poop-deck), where it is attached to the tiller. From this position atop the deck, the post passes through open space underneath the deck, then through the bottom of the hull and continues along the aft edge of the deadwood, until it reaches the bottom of the deadwood, where it is supported by a gudgeon, which is attached to the deadwood. That plan was modified by Beaton's, so that the rudderpost does not extend above the rear deck.

Fig. 71

In fig. 71 (preceding page) we see the rear of Ghost. The port and starboard bilge stringers are visible running along the sides of the cockpit floor. The rudderpost is seen in the middle toward the rear of the floor. It does not rise to the height of the deck, which has been cut back, so that the rear of the cockpit is more open than it would be, had Sweisguth's design been followed. The tiller will be attached to the post and hinged upward in order that is easily grasped by the helmsman (see below ch. II.6.3).

Fig. 72

The rudderpost passes downward from the floor of the cockpit, running along the rear of the deadwood, which has been shaped (made concave) to accept a round post. At the bottom of the deadwood, it is supported by a bronze gudgeon (fig. 72), whose size and shape are unique. It is A Cat specific and not available from makers of marine hardware, so that Beaton's made a wooden pattern, from which a bronze fitting was cast and machined. The gudgeon was subsequently attached to Ghost, being placed in a form-fitting (rectangular) depression at the end of the deadwood. In the photo we see the gudgeon in place, where it is being secured by rivets.

Fig. 73

Rudderblades can be made from a single piece of wood, which is normal for smaller boats like Sail Fish and Duck Boats, but given the size of the A Cat rudder and the pressures on the rudder when the boat alters course, the craftsmen at Beaton's prefer a laminated construction involving two pieces of mahogany plywood, bronze bolts, epoxy glue and glass cloth (fig. 73).

One way to proceed—the way preferred by Paul Smith—is for slots to be cut in each of two pieces of plywood. These slots are for bolts that attach the rudderblade to the rudderpost. One piece of plywood is laid flat on a table with the slots for bolts facing up. Bolts with the rudderpost already attached are then placed in the slots, in such a way that the post is positioned against the forward edge of the plywood, i.e., what will become the forward edge of the rudder. After that epoxy glue is applied to the plywood and a layer of reinforcing glass cloth is laid down. It is saturated with epoxy. Next the inner face of the other piece of plywood is coated with epoxy and positioned above the first piece of plywood, so that the slots cut for bolts are atop the bolts. Nuts and washers are now put on the bolt ends through holes previously cut in the plywood. The nuts are tightened slightly and the plywood sandwich is clamped down as flat and straight as possible. After that the nuts are further tightened.

Fig. 74

A second way to proceed is quite similar to the first and involves the bronze bolts. It is suggested by the photo, which shows the rudder already made into a sandwich. It is leaning against a support and standing on its rear edge, i.e., what will become the aft edge of the rudder. The bronze bolts, which will attach the rudder to the post, can be seen at the bottom of the photo. All four of the bolts have been inserted into the post and each carries a nut. At the top of the photo one sees wooden dowels serving as placeholders for the bolts. They will be removed and the bronze bolts will be inserted, the nuts having been removed. The ends of the bolts will reach the squares already cut in the mahogany plywood, so that nuts and washers can be affixed to the ends and tightened in order to solidify the construct. After that the combination, rudder and post, will be attached to the deadwood, so that Ghost will have a rudder properly positioned underneath and at the rear of the hull.

From the photo it seems likely that the construction of Ghost's rudder and its placement aft of the deadwood proceeded in the second way. But however the procedure progressed, the different colors seen on the rudder reflect the layered makeup of plywood. In the case of Ghost, the plywood has eight layers, in which the grain runs in different directions. That makes not only for strength but also for variation in color. Ghost's rudder is tapered toward the rear (in the photo that is the bottom) in order to create a smooth flow of water, i.e., from front to rear. The tapering proceeds across eight different grains which repeatedly change direction. In the darker sections the grain is running up and down (in the photo that is sideways) and in the lighter sections the grain is running sideways (in the photo up and down).

If the photo is turned sideways, it becomes clear how the rudder fits under the boat. The lead edge of the rudder, together with the post to which it is attached, slants forward as it progresses downward along the rear edge of the deadwood (see Sweisguth's designs ch. II.2 figs. 8-10). That has two consequences. First, it creates a modicum of space between the top of the rudder and the bottom of the hull. When the rudder is turned hard one way or the other, that space is narrowed, so that occasionally the rudder makes contact with the bottom. It might even become stuck, but that is rare and a black mark against the builder.

Second, the bottom of the rudder is not aligned with the deadwood. Its rear edge is noticeably lower, and in shallow water it will hit ground—thick muck on Barnegat Bay—before the deadwood does. That can cause damage to the rudder, as happened to Ghost during its first season. The occasion was a Sunday race off Shore Acres, when the rudder hit ground. The crew felt the hit but continued to focus on the race, after which Ghost was towed back to Beaton's, where it had a slip on the main dock. The next day Bill returned to check on the boat and discovered that the tiller moved without resistance. The rudder had fallen off and floated away. The time lag between hitting ground and the disappearance of the rudder was and still is difficult to explain, but at the time that mattered little. Ghost needed a rudder for Saturday's BBYRA race. Beaton's response exceeded expectations. The woodshop was able to cobble together a temporary replacement for Saturday's race, and in the weeks that followed a permanent rudder was made, which did not descend below the deadwood. It would survive shallow water (ch. VIII.1 end).

The shape of the rudder in Sweisguth's designs, both that of March and that of November, is of some interest, for the rear is curved, which is common on smaller boats like the Lightning and the Comet. Ghost's first rudder was similar in that it too was curved, but not so round as the rudder drawn by Sweisguth. Rather, the curvature was limited to the top and the bottom of the rear edge (see fig. 74). Ghost's second rudder departed even more from Sweisguth's design: it assumed a more rectangular shape. The back edge became straight and tapered, while the top and bottom were straight and largely parallel to each other. As stated, the bottom edge no longer dipped below the deadwood, and by not rounding the corners of the rear edge some additional area will have been gained, but not much. Whether that enhanced steering is doubtful.

3) The Tiller

The tiller connects to the rudderpost and is used by the helmsman to steer the boat. Since the rudderpost in the drawings of Sweisguth rises above the rear deck, the tiller need not be hinged to the rudderpost in such a way that it inclines sharply upward to the helmsman, when he is seated and sailing to weather. Indeed, Sweisguth's drawings show only the slightest incline (ch. II.2 figs. 8-10). That is not true of Ghost, for there the rudderpost rises no higher than the floor boards (see above fig. 71). That may be viewed as a mark of Beaton's independence: Sweisguth's drawings need not be followed in all details. But it would be a mistake to think that in lowering the height of the rudderpost, the craftsmen at Beaton's engaged in innovation. In fact, they were following the lead of Charles Mower, who in designing the first A Cat, namely Mary Ann, called for a rudderpost that rises no higher than the floor (see "American Catboats" p. 95).

Being attached to the rudderpost at floor level, Ghost's tiller is necessarily hinged, so that it rises upward to reach the helmsman. And if that is true when the helmsman is seated sailing to weather, it is even truer when the helmsman is standing while steering downwind. Moreover, since the rudderpost is no longer passing through the rear deck, the deck can be shortened and the area remaining under the deck can become a storage area. In the photo reproduced above (fig. 71), one sees the transom closed off. If one looks closely, the outline of an entry to the closed off area is apparent. It would soon be cut and a removable door made. In practice, Ghost rarely sailed with that door in place or even on board. It was an extra that could get in the way, and in any case the enclosed area needed to be ventilated.

A Cats can have a strong weather helm, which the helmsman must use strength to resist. So too the tiller itself must be able to resist bending and breaking under severe pressure. That made black locust (sometimes called yellow locust) a suitable wood for the tiller. For it is coarse-grained, hard and exceptionally durable in contact with wet weather. In addition, black locust is not only strong but also attractive in color when sanded and varnished.

In fig. 75, Russ Manheimer is seen sanding the tiller in preparation for a second or third coat of varnish. The tiller is tapered. It is thickest at the end to which the rudderpost is attached and becomes thinner as it moves away from the post. But the taper is gradual and slight. The strength of the tiller is not compromised. The taper ends in a round ball that might be viewed as decorative but it is also functional. It serves as a stop that prevents the helmsman's hand or hands from sliding off the tiller.

In addition, it gives the helmsman a place to grab the tiller with his full fist, should he wish to stand up or simply steer with one hand. That said, most helmsmen use two hands, sitting on the weather bench and turning their head to look forward. At least that was normal when Ghost was built. Not a few years later, a new shape was introduced. The ball at the end of the tiller was replaced by a kind of handle. Across from the helmsman's position, the tiller divides in two, forms parallel, horizontal curves and then comes together again at the end, leaving an opening approximately one foot long. Some skippers find the new design a significant improvement. At very least they do not need to lean over so far or sit on the edge of the bench in order to reach the tiller. But Ghost never made the change. Bill preferred sitting close to the tiller and using two hands. That a race was ever decided by the shape of the tiller is hard to believe.

Fig. 75

7. Cabin Doors

Earlier in ch. II.5.4, the focus was on the cabin. Reference was made to the construction of entryways into the cabin and to the doors that belong to these entries. Discussion of the doors was postponed, since the doors can be viewed as extra items, which are not essential to an A Cat. Indeed, doors have not been built for the most recent A Cats. That is understandable, for doors are an additional expense and of little use in a boat whose primary purpose is racing on weekends. Back at its slip or mooring, having doors to lock might be a safeguard against thieves, but on Barnegat Bay thieves are rare. And more importantly, closing the doors will seriously impede ventilating the cabin.

Not surprisingly, Ghost raced without doors in place, and at rest in its slip at the Bay Head Yacht Club, it was not protected against intruders by locked doors. Rather, the entryways were left open, in order that the air blowing through the windscoop on the foredeck could pass through the cabin and have a drying effect. Nevertheless, doors were built for Ghost, and on special days—Fourth of July, Labor Day and Birthdays—they were a welcome embellishment.

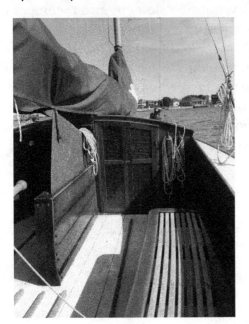
Fig. 76

Fig. 77

The photographs above in ch. II.5.4 (figs. 64 and 65) give some idea of the careful work done by Mark Dawson in preparing the side panels for the hanging of doors. Here now are two photographs of the doors hanging in place (figs. 76 and 77). The photos reflect the fact that the doors were not finished in time for the launching on

June 12 (1994); indeed, they were not finished for another month, when Ghost was already fitted out for racing. Hence, in the photos one sees Ghost afloat with lines draped over the centerboard to the left of the starboard pair of doors and with halyards hung on cleats to the right of the doors.

The doors were made by Russ Manheimer. There are two doors for each entryway, and each door has two panels, which are held in place by frames made of African mahogany. The panels are made of sapele plywood, which is light in weight and also attractive—appears traditional—when framed. The joining of panels and frames was accomplished by cutting slots in the mahogany frames, the slots being of such a width that they accepted both the plywood panels and simple tenons that were cut on the ends of the horizontal frames. That created a rigid and warp free door.

Ventilation slots were cut into the plywood panels by using a table saw set at an angle that would keep out rain but still permit air to flow in and out of the cabin. Together with two windows, one on each side of the cabin, and an air scoop forward of the cabin, the airflow would make the cabin comfortable for overnighting, providing mosquitoes could be kept out. Since the side windows had screening and the air scoop could easily be fitted with a temporary piece of screening, it remained only to acquire screens that would fit over the ventilation slots cut into the upper panels of the doors. The screening would be attached to the inside of the doors, in order not to detract from the doors, when they are viewed from the cockpit or dock. And the screening would be removable. But screening was never acquired. After Ghost's disastrous first race (see ch.VI.1), everyone was focused on racing and not on an extra like screening. To be sure, there were occasional jokes concerning overnighting in a marshy area well removed from envious eyes, but that never happened. At least not in the early years, when the crew of Ghost had a single focus.

III
OIL, PAINT AND VARNISH

1. Preparation and Application

Wooden boats require oil, paint and varnish not only for appearance but also for preservation. Ghost is no exception. At various times during construction, Ghost's hull, its spars, rudder and tiller were carefully prepared by sanding and/or cleaning, after which various finishes were applied. For example, before the cabin had been completed but after the coaming was in place (ch. II.5), multiple coats of an oil finish were brushed on the planks and ribs that were exposed inside the hull. The finish can be a custom mix of boiled linseed oil and organic solvent or a commercial product such as Deks Olje. This procedure prevents water absorption, which adds unwanted weight to the hull. To be sure, clear days with plenty of sunshine can help dry out an interior, but repeated soaking followed by drying, expansion and contraction, would over time weaken the wood and lead to deterioration.

Fig. 78

In fig. 78, we see Mark Dawson on his knees applying oil, which would penetrate the wood and mitigate the effects of bilge water. Above Mark, the mahogany wood used in making sides for the cabin and coaming for the cockpit is now in place. A join created by scarfing (see ch. II.5.2 with fig. 56) can be seen to the left of Mark. But the cabin remains to be enclosed.

Bent over and on his knees, Mark looks a tad uncomfortable, but his task would have been more difficult, were he working within the finished cabin, cramped between roofing and floorboards that are separated by gaps to permit ventilation. The vacuum cleaner that is visible at the bottom of the photo tells us that the area being oiled was cleaned—dust and wood chips were removed—before the oiling began.

The deck and the cabin top will be painted, but first they needed to be finished, i.e., covered with xynole and sealed with epoxy. That accomplished (see ch. II.5.4 with figs. 68 and 69), they were painted an off-white. For a light color would minimize the heat that a dark color would generate when exposed to bright sun.

Fig. 79

In fig. 79, the hull is shown with the waterline scribed and the hull fully sanded. The topsides above the waterline are covered with a light blue primer. Several coats of primer will be applied before the rub rails are fastened in place. Concerning the props supporting the boat from underneath, see above ch. II.3.3 with fig.30.

Fig. 80

Not only have the topsides been primed but also the rub rails and toe rails have been fit and fastened in place (fig. 80). Holes for fasteners in rails have been plugged and sanded.

In fig. 81 on the next page, we see Ghost from the rear. The transom as well as the rub and toe rails have been sanded and stained with Interlux #42 Brown Mahogany. At least one coat of varnish has been applied. The varnished surfaces usually have from

Fig. 81

eight to ten coats of varnish when completed. The deadwood surface shows areas of fairing compound that will be sanded for a smooth base, to which primer and anti-fouling paint will be applied (see fig. 85).

Fig. 82

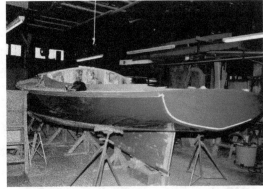

Fig. 83

In figs. 82 and 83, the hull above the waterline, which had already received a light blue primer (figs. 79 and 80), has now been coated with a dark green enamel sometimes referred to as British racing green—think of the sporty MG that seated two persons—or more humbly as forest green. Apparently Bozo the cat approved. Instead of keeping vigil (see ch. II.1 with fig. 7), the mouser can be seen enjoying a pleasant snooze.

Fig. 84

Exceptional is the transom. It is made from a single piece of mahogany (see ch. II.3.3 with fig. 25) and has received multiple coats of varnish. Sanding occurred between each new coat (fig. 81). Now the transom carries the name "Ghost," hand lettered in gold leaf (fig. 84).

The aft portion of the deadwood is seen below the transom. A semicircular recess has been cut into the aft end. It will accept the rod to which the rudder will be attached. The gudgeon, which will hold the rudder from below, is held in place by a clamp. A rivet can be seen sticking out of the gudgeon, but it needs to be peened (see ch. II.6.2 with fig. 72).

For the bottom below the waterline including the rudder and deadwood, class rules called for an antifouling paint. Preparation included sanding the bottom of the hull and smoothing the deadwood. The latter was made of layered pieces of mahogany, which is an open grain wood. That called for applying a paste wood-filler (see fig. 81) followed by a thorough sanding. In fig. 85, Russ is seen sitting on the floor beneath Ghost applying paste. The rudder has yet to be attached and the bronze gudgeon in which it will sit is still held by a clamp.

Fig. 85

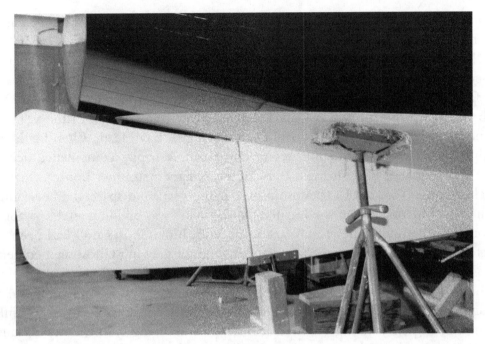

Fig. 86

Anti-fouling paint is often reddish. That is the mark of a copper base, which makes bottom paint quite soft. In the case of Ghost, a slightly harder but still legal paint was chosen. It had an ablative quality, which made the bottom largely (but not entirely) self-cleaning. Chosen was a light color that in the accompanying photo appears white. Note that the gudgeon and with it the rudder are now in place, but the gudgeon is still held by a clamp. The open holes await rivets.

Like the transom, the mast and boom also received multiple coats of varnish (see ch. IV.2 with fig. 89); so too the tiller (see ch. II.6 with fig.75).

2. Traditional Colors

The decision to paint the deck off-white and the topsides dark green was in line with Bill Fortenbaugh's practice over many years. In the 1940s Bill's Duck Boat had been white on the deck and dark green below. In the 1950s his Sneakbox was entirely green, top and bottom. And his G Sloop, had a white deck, green topsides and a bottom covered with anti-fouling paint, whose color varied from season to season. Even his M Scows and E Scows conformed to this pattern. Indeed, in choosing colors for Ghost, Bill was opting to follow a tradition that was not only his but also predated him. For dark green had long been a color of choice on Barnegat Bay. It was suited to boats that were used for hunting ducks—it provided a measure of camouflage—and was attractive to the eye when seen against the brown waters of the Bay.

Nevertheless, the choice of dark green for Ghost's topsides had an unexpected consequence, when Bill took Catherine "Dood" Barnett to see Ghost at Beaton's. Her father was Frank Thacher, who had been a member of the Seaside Park Yacht Club and the owner of two A Cats, Helen and Spy (see ch. I.1). In the year 1926, he and his family left Seaside to begin summering in Bay Head. When he died, his family continued to spend summers in Bay Head. A happy coincidence occurred in 1943, when Sam Fortenbaugh, Bill's father, bought a summer house next to the Thacher house. That led to friendship over many years and sparked a keen interest on the part of Dood, when she learned that Beaton's was building an A Cat for Bill. Accordingly, he invited her to visit Beaton's with him. Ghost's hull had been constructed and the topsides painted green. The time for viewing Ghost seemed perfect. Bill also invited Betty Kellogg to join them, for Betty was a close friend of Dood and had known Bill's mother. Moreover, Betty's son Peter was having another A Cat, Vapor, built in Philadelphia. What ensued was a striking example of a mother thinking of her child. Upon entering the shed at Beaton's and seeing Ghost, Betty exclaimed, "That's Peter's color." There must have been a short pause before Bill responded, but he soon understood that Betty would not have been familiar with his own traditional choice of colors let alone the use of green that was common in earlier times. He offered a succinct explanation, and what had been a startling exclamation quickly became a non-event. The three were soon talking about shades of green and the color of the Kellogg's G Sloop.

IV
SPARS AND SAILS

1. Two Sweisguth Plans: the Sail

In the opening chapter of this book (I.1) and again in the second chapter (II.2), mention was made of Francis Sweisguth, who designed Tamwock in 1923 for Francis Larkin. That boat was later destroyed by fire but details concerning the spars and sail have survived on two designs or drawings. One is labeled "Sail Plan" and records the date as March 1923. The other is called "New Sail Plan" and gives the date November 1923. In this chapter, the designs are printed side by side on the facing pages that follow (figs. 87 and 88). They are precious documents, for viewed together, they illustrate how Sweisguth participated in the evolution of the A Cat Class.

Most striking is the appearance of the so-called "Swedish" rig—a wooden spar or gaff at the top of the sail—on the design drawn in March, and its disappearance from the design drawn in November. Apparently the racing season of 1923 had shown the Swedish rig to be of no value or worse in competition against Mary Ann, which was fitted out with a Marconi rig. As a consequence the Swedish rig was abandoned. Beginning 1924, all A Cats would exhibit a Marconi rig.

To be sure, there were and still are occasions when a gaff rig may be preferred. For example, when masts were regularly made out of a single piece of wood, it might be difficult to find tall straight trees, which could become usable masts. It was easier to extend the height by means of a gaff and thereby increase the sail area. Moreover, when a mast is of one piece and of considerable height, a low fixed bridge blocks passage. To be sure, one could remove the mast, but with tall masts that is impractical. It would be better to have a gaff that can be lowered, thereby increasing the number of bridges that can be passed under with ease. True enough, but bridges were of little concern to the owners of the first A Cats. What did interest the owners was winning races, and toward that end the Marconi rig was preferred. It eliminates unwanted weight above. Not only is the wooden gaff gone but also the wire stay, which on Sweisguth's March plan is held off the mast by means of a bronze strut. Moreover, there is little loss in sail area. On the November plan, the head of the sail now extends to the top of the mast 45 feet 4 inches above the deck: i.e., it extends to the highest sheave, which in the March plan serves as a conduit through which the rake of the

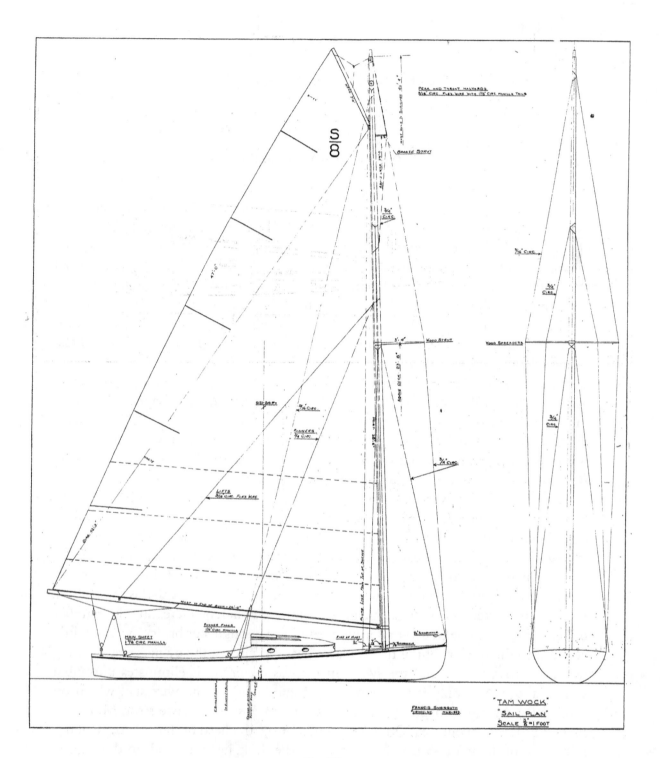

Fig. 87

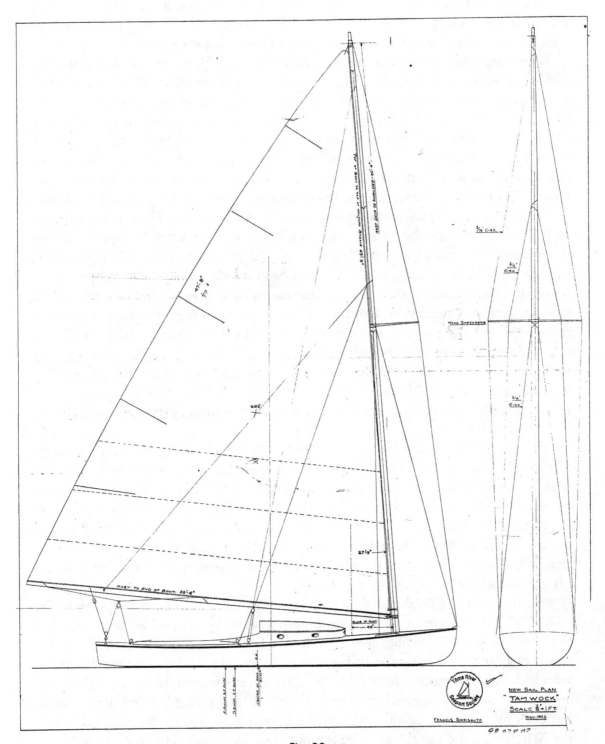

Fig. 88

gaff is controlled. In addition, the boom is extended from 26 feet six inches to 28 feet four inches. As a result, the leech is increased from 47 feet to 47 feet eight inches. And without the gaff at the top of the sail, leech control is improved.

There are other differences that may be mentioned. Here are four. 1) Both plans announce the same scale: three eighths of an inch equals one foot. Were that adhered to, the overall length of the boat in the November plan would be two-thirds of a foot longer. But the plans are announced as sail plans so that exactness in the length of the hull is not a concern. 2) The top of the cabin in the March plan exhibits a sliding cover. It is not present in the November plan. Again the difference is unimportant in drawings whose focus is the sail. 3) The mast in the November plan exhibits a greater rake aft. That is more interesting, for in combination with the longer boom and longer leech, it affects the sail and suggests a concern with helm and the ability to point high upwind. 4) Only the March plan shows insignia. The letter "S" appears above the numeral "8" with a horizontal bar separating the two. The letter refers to Seaside Park and the numeral distinguishes the boat from others hailing from the same port. What is curious is the position and size of the insignia: toward the very top of the sail and small in comparison with the size of the sail. Photographs from the period make clear that the position and size were normal for the time, but that still leaves one wondering. To be sure, being small requires less stitching—no stick-on insignia in the nineteen twenties—and were the insignia placed lower where the sail is much wider, a larger size would require more stitching. Be that as it may, what we can say is that the failure to repeat the insignia in November is unimportant in a plan drawn by a naval architect.

In both the March and November plans, a front-on drawing appears to the right of the sail plan. It is wildly out of proportion: indeed, in the absence of a deep and heavily weighted keel, so tall a mast with sail hoisted would soon cause such a narrow hull to roll over and fill with water. But that can be ignored as irrelevant to the sail plans. What Sweisguth intends to show is not only the shape and area of the sail but also the number of side and fore stays, the points on the mast to which they are attached, and the positions of the bronze strut (March design only) and the wooden spreaders, both sideways and forward facing.

Finally it should be noted that both the March and November plans refer to "TAM WOCK" in uppercase letters and with a space in the middle suggesting that the name of the boat divides into two words. But that is not the case. The word "tamwock" (no division) refers to the cod (fish) and was chosen by Francis Larkin, who had made his money dealing in cod. That leaves one wondering how the error arose and why it was repeated some eight months later. In regard to repetition, mindless copying from the earlier design to the later is a possibility. But that still leaves the March plan, and can the error be attributed to Sweisguth? His contemporaneous hull plans, both the March and November plans (II.2), have "Tamwock," one word.

Perhaps a later hand introduced error into the sail plans. Be that as it may, the word "tamwock" (lowercase) is not in everybody's vocabulary, so that it may be helpful to cite, e.g., the Standard Dictionary of Facts (1922 p. 809), where we are told that "tamwock" is the American Indian word for codfish. More authoritative is Roger Williams, *A Key to the American Language* 1643, fifth edition 1936 p.111, where we read "Pauganaùt, tamwock." The two words are to be understood as synonyms. (See the last page [unnumbered] of Williams' introduction.) The accompanying explanation runs "*Cod*, Which is the first that comes a little before the Spring." The word in italics is the translation; the rest is descriptive. In Williams' text lack of space causes the word "tamwock" to be divided into two syllables: "tam" and "wock." Nevertheless, we are not to believe that Sweisguth was influenced by the division occurring in Williams' text. What we can say is that Sweisguth's division of "tamwock" is syllabically correct.

2. Mast and Boom

Fig. 89   Fig. 90

Mary Ann benefitted not only from a Marconi rig but also from the use of Sitka spruce and modern glues. Combining these materials, Pidgeon Hollow Spars in Boston constructed a mast that was light in weight, c. 47 feet tall and flexible. The mast was built in two sections, which were hollowed out and firmly glued together. The sections were then tapered and rounded to its finished shape. The first A Cat masts built by Beaton's were of similar design, except that they were laminated from thinner boards of spruce and held together with West epoxy glue. Ghost's mast was of this construction. It was quite flexible, and when supported by stays it permitted the crew on Ghost to make changes according to the velocity of the wind.

In fig. 89, we see Russ varnishing the foot of Ghost's mast. The rectangular piece sticking out at the very bottom fits into the maststep, i.e., a slot below deck on top of the keel (see II.3.2 with fig. 16). We might speak of mortise and tenon construction, providing we do not think of a tight fitting join that leaves no room for movement. In the case of Ghost's mast, the slot is slightly longer than the rectangular piece. That permits adjustment fore and aft, which determines in part the rake of the mast. The opening in the deck forward of the cabin (see ch. II.3.5 with fig. 42), through which the mast passes, also permits adjustment. In both cases, wedges or chocks will be inserted to fix the mast firmly in the desired position.

In fig. 90, Ghost's mast has already been glued and fitted out with spreaders and stays. We see Russ Manheimer working at the foot of the mast. The windows to the main shed are open suggesting a warm day in late spring 1994. The launching of Ghost was scheduled to occur on June 12, but it was not necessary that the mast be entirely ready and in place for that occasion. A "stump" would be used to support decorative pennants (ch. V.2). For photos of the mast being stepped, see ch. VI.1.

The original booms for A Cats were built by Morton Johnson in Bay Head. They were solid and either round or rectangular in shape. In time, hollow booms were introduced to save weight. Ghost's original boom was hollow, round, and tapered toward the rear.

On the opposite page, in fig. 91 we see Ghost in a photo dated 1995. The flexibility of the spars is striking. Ghost's mast is not only raked slightly aft but also bending (put a straightedge to the picture). The bend in the boom is more obvious. Both contribute to flattening the sail in heavy wind. The bend in the mast will loosen the leech, so that the wind flows more smoothly off the rear of the sail, thereby eliminating or at least mitigating a weather helm that would slow the boat. The bend in the boom, along with the bend in the mast will reduce the pocket/draft in the sail and in that way flatten the sail. In the photo, the wind does not appear to be strong, but if it increases bending the spars will be helpful. In a real blow, however, reefing the sail becomes all but necessary.

The line toward bottom of the sail and running fore and aft is marked by holes through which lines or ties pass when the sail is reefed (see ch. IV.3). Worth noting is the hole that is most forward, being up against the bolt rope. It is strengthened by a bronze ring and repeated below closer to the boom. Both rings are connected to a piece of cloth that is dark and runs diagonally upward. It adds reinforcement. In the case of the upper ring, that is additional to the reinforcement provided by the corner patch. In the case of the lower ring, the reinforcement is not additional. Rather, it provides modest reinforcement, should the ring be used as a "Cunningham hole," when reefing seems unnecessary, but tightening the luff seems desirable. In that way, the camber in the sail is pulled nearer the luff and the leech is made flatter.

Sometime after the year 2000 and hence after Ghost's seven consecutive Bay championships, a rectangular/box style boom was built for Ghost. Most likely the decision to abandon the original boom should be attributed to a "herd" mentality,

Fig. 91

for most if not the whole fleet was making the change to the box shaped boom. But whatever the motive, the new boom seemed to make no difference to Ghost's performance.

3. Sails

While Ghost was under construction, two sails were made in anticipation of the 1994 racing season. One sail was intended for heavy winds; the other for use in most conditions. The former was made by Skip Moorhouse in Moorestown, New Jersey. The sail was well built, but exceptionally heavy and flat. It was used once and then put aside. The other sail was made by Mark Beaton. It was unquestionably fast and would be used throughout the first season and well into the second.

Mark is the son of Ted Beaton and cousin of Tom. He learned to make sails by working for Henry Bossett, who was an outstanding sailor on Barnegat Bay. Oldsters remember his dominance in the M Scow class, while others think of him as a champion in both the iceboat and catamaran classes. Bossett began making sails in North Jersey, but in the mid-1980s he moved his business to Point Pleasant. There Mark began an apprenticeship, which taught him the importance of "sweating the details." No sail was built to the wrong dimension or fitted out with slides too large or too small. As Mark tells it, "those kinds of mistakes simply did not happen."

Fig. 92

In March of 1988, Mark opened his own business in the loft above the wood-shop at Beaton's. In the photo, we see Mark leaning against the edge of the cavity, in which he sits to sew. The room around him is not especially large, but the available floor space is sufficient for laying out A Cat sails, parts or whole, which can then be dragged to the sewing machine for stitching. Hence, when Bill Fortenbaugh came to ask about making a sail for Ghost—the boat was already being built in the wood-shop below—Mark thought that he could undertake the project and agreed to do so. Another sailmaker might have declined, for the project was by no means simple and would be accomplished the old fashioned way, i.e., without a computer program.

The old-fashioned way means drawing a full-size outline of the sail on the floor, over which panels of cloth are laid, being placed perpendicular to the leech and crossing the luff and foot at a diagonal. The panels are overlapped by the width of the seams plus the amount needed for broadseaming, i.e., for tapering the edges of the panels, thereby achieving fullness or camber in the body of the sail. In this way, the position of the draft is determined. And that is important, for if the draft is too far aft, it will create a leech that is tighter than desired: one which will cause drag and result in a weather helm. And if the draft is too far forward, the boat will fall short in its ability to point high when sailing upwind.

Before the panels are removed from the floor, marks are made showing the locations of batten pockets, the positions of reef points and the edges of the sail. Later in completing the sail, the batten pockets are sewn on and the panels are sewn together. Corner reinforcements are added, the edges are finished, and sail slides and corner rings are put in place. As a final step, the sail insignia are pasted on the sail. In the case of Ghost, the insignia are "BH G." The letters "BH" stand for Bay Head and "G" for Ghost. In later years, when designs became popular and replaced letters on A Cat sails, Ghost might have opted for the drawing of a ghost, e.g., of Casper (see below), but Ghost continued to identify itself with "BH G," thereby signaling loyalty to the Bay Head Yacht Club and at the same time expressing delight in spooking the competition.

In the years that followed, Mark and Bill shared ideas, which led to changes in production and product. One area that had proved troublesome was the structure of batten pockets. Smaller one-design sails usually feature an elastic strap sewn inside the front end of the pocket. That holds the batten back tight against the leech. This system is very effective on shorter battens like those of an E Scow, Comet or Lightning. But on the six-foot long battens of an A Cat, that system does not work. The elastic cannot generate enough force to hold the batten in place, so that a batten can become dislodged when the boat is under sail in strong wind and rough water. Eventually a pocket design was settled on. It features webbing at the front end of the pocket, against which the batten bears. Tension is applied at the leech end by means of a webbing strap that folds over the aft end of the batten and is secured with a Velcro closure, which is able to hold the batten in place.

Another area that received attention was the design and construction of corner patches, which serve as reinforcements. These patches are highly visible and can be seen either as an integral part of the design or as an afterthought. In time a design was settled on that was attractive and at the same time provided the requisite strength. Other refinements included extending the top batten to the luff and routing the leech cord up to the head of the sail and then down along the luff to where it could be tightened or loosened as desired.

There were, of course, changes that were deemed unnecessary or ill-advised and subsequently abandoned. An example of the former was adding a line of extra cloth to strengthen the area between reef points (see IV.2 fig. 91). That was not a new idea and seemed sensible, for when reefing is done in haste the ties that secure the shortened sail to the boom are often uneven, so that tension is not evenly distributed along the sail. That might have become standard, if reefing were a weekly event. But it was not, so that adding the line of cloth was soon deemed unnecessary.

An example of an ill-advised change was using plastic slides along the luff in an attempt to save weight. Under load, the plastic slides deformed causing them to pop off the track. Startling, to say the least, and requiring an emergency drop of the sail. A different, eye-popping example—and one which Mark observed but never tried—was making a sail with full-length battens and an extended roach that went well beyond the line from head to clew. The sail area was greatly increased, but the extra area did not prove to be an advantage. Moreover, the extra sailcloth and super long battens were awkward to work with and so irritating. That demonstrated ever so clearly that not all changes, even clever changes, are improvements. And more importantly, it made clear that the A Cat Class needed to expand and tighten its rules, so that owners and sailmakers alike do not seek an advantage, whatever the cost might be. Today that need has been largely met, while still allowing room for some creativity.

After several years of cutting sails by hand, Mark upgraded to an electronic system called Prosail, which allowed him to refine his designs and cut sails with a high degree of accuracy. The system had been developed in New Zealand and could be put to use in Mark's loft, thereby saving considerable time and effort. But, of course, technology did not come to a halt, and the global economy took sail making off shore. Today Mark sends his files to a "super-loft" in, e.g., China, the Philippines or Sri Lanka, where sails are cut out, stitched and finished. After that the sails are sent to Mark for inspection, insignia, battens and delivery. One might complain that the romance of sail-making has been diminished, but among A Cat sailors Mark's reputation as the leading supplier of winning sails remains intact. His loft is still the go-to place.

Mark's contribution to Ghost's success was not limited to supplying the sails that powered Ghost to seven consecutive Bay Championships. He was also willing to come aboard on race day. He regularly offered sound advice on sail trim, and on occasion he did not hesitate to call out the skipper. When he observed Bill pinching upwind

Fig. 93

and slowing the boat to no advantage, he would say succinctly, "Bear off and keep the boat moving." Indeed, in 1996, on the day that Vapor challenged Ghost for the Bay championship, Mark was aboard Ghost and did his part to ensure victory (ch. VI.2).

Fig. 94

Finally, a nice touch! Since A Cat sails are quite large, they are not removed and bagged after each sail or race. Rather, they are left still attached to mast and boom, carefully folded or rolled and covered with a synthetic material that offers protection against sun and rain. Ghost is no exception. Mark provided a well-fitting sail cover that was dark green to match Ghost's hull. And forward near the mast, on both the port and starboard sides, there was sewn onto the cloth a white Ghost, which was often compared with the cartoon character known to all as Casper the Friendly Ghost.

The idea came from Mark's assistant Roberta Schreyer, who used to appear on Friday afternoons to watch and encourage the crew of Ghost as they cleaned the boat's bottom and topsides in anticipation of Saturday's BBYRA race. Over the years, Roberta's ghost evoked numerous happy responses, smiles and cheerful words, not only among Ghost's crew but also among competitors and random visitors to the docks at Bay Head.

In fig. 94, we see the port side of the boat. To the left of the Ghost figure, there is a patch that identifies the cover as the product of Beaton Sails. The photo was taken after Ghost's last race at the LEHYC in 2015. Lined up are Bill, Mark Kotzas, Dave Hoder, Robert Wahlers, and Greg Matzat. For a second photo taken after the one shown here, see ch. VII.2 fig. 150.

V.

THE LAUNCHING

1. Out of the Shed for Viewing

Early in the morning of June twelfth, Ghost was ready to be moved out of Beaton's main shed, the woodshop, in which she had been built and painted. Many things that still needed to be done—cleats affixed to the deck, the mast stepped, the boom attached and much else—would be accomplished in the open air, once Ghost had been christened and was afloat in the basin.

The move began within the woodshop by sliding a low two-wheeled trailer under Ghost. In fig. 95, the trailer is already under Ghost. Her bow is supported by a single block, which will soon be replaced by a wooden cradle-like support. That will help prevent rocking as the trailer is pulled over rough spots in the driveway outside the shop. Russ Manheimer is busy toward the rear of the trailer.

Fig. 95

Fig. 96

Fig. 97

Once the boat was properly supported both fore and aft, the trailer was attached to a tractor driven by Tom Beaton (not shown) and towed out of the shed to the launching area (fig. 96). There Tom used the tractor to back Ghost under the yard's travel lift on rails. Slings were passed under the boat, which was then lifted off the trailer. In fig. 97, we see Ghost resting in the slings. She was soon moved a short distance backwards to a position near the water, where the baptism would take place later in the afternoon. In the background one can see the rigging ladder, which on another day would be used to put Ghost's mast in place (see ch.VI.1).

Ghost was set down in close proximity to the water. The slings were removed and spectators began to crowd around Ghost in order to view up close her hull and cockpit. Remarkably little room was left for persons wishing to inspect Ghost's transom. In hindsight it seems a matter of good fortune that no one viewing the transom took an extra step backwards and fell into the water (fig. 98).

Fig. 98

No one counted heads, but a conservative estimate is that over a three-hour period two hundred fifty persons were present, many of whom witnessed the event in its entirety. They included the craftsmen who had built Ghost for Bill (see fig. 99 on next page), in which Bill appears together with Michael Delorme, Russ Manheimer, Tom Beaton and Mark Dawson; missing from the photo is Paul Smith, who was ailing with a bad leg and could be present at the event only briefly (for a photo of Paul at work, see ch. II.3.3 fig. 26.). In addition, the crew of Ghost was present, as were family

Fig. 99

and friends of the crew, persons who would soon be competing against Ghost, and curious persons who hailed from the several yacht clubs that constitute the BBYRA.

Fig 100 provides a look inside Ghost's cockpit. In particular, it shows the two entrances into the cabin with the centerboard trunk in the middle (see ch. II.5.4 with figs. 64 and 65). The centerboard is raised and so visible above the trunk. It is painted a dark green to match the topsides. The doors to the cabin have not yet been made. That will happen in the weeks after the racing begins. See ch. II.7.

Fig. 100

As often at launchings, Ghost's proper mast had not been set in place. Instead, Ghost received a stub-mast, from which a line ran fore and aft and on which blue, red and white pennants were tied. They were decoration but also more. They had been won by Bill over many years and represent first, second and third place finishes in races sponsored both by the Bay Head Yacht Club for its members and by the BBYRA for member clubs. In figs. 100 and 101, the pennants in front of the stub-mast exhibit a blue star, which refers to the BHYC. "M" is an abbreviation for "M Scow", "G" for G Sloop, and "Snk" for "Sneakbox" On the pennants aft of stub, the initials are those of clubs belonging to the BBYRA: e.g., "OGYC" for "Ocean Gate," "SAYC" for "Shore Acres" and "TRYC" for "Toms River".

Notable in fig. 101 is the bottle of Rheingold beer, which appears to the left of the mother and child. It is sitting on a Rheingold tray and raised up on a block to protect it from a clumsy spectator. The proximity of the bottle to the boat is a not too subtle reminder that the crew of Ghost had adopted Rheingold as its power drink (see II.4). The lady to the right looking up with neck bent back might mislead one into thinking that Ghost's tall mast is in place. But that would be a mistaken impression, attributable to the angle at which the photo is taken.

Fig. 101

2. The Ceremony: Speech, Verse, and Song

GHOST
gets her bottom wet

A Traditional, Funfilled
LAUNCHING

at
DAVID BEATON & SONS
on
JUNE 12, 1994

music from 2:00 PM
by the Sea Breeze
Ghost's favorite beer and the world's best rye for the drinking

The Ceremony at 3:00 PM

Kearney Kuhlthau: My Beer is Rheingold the Dry Beer

> **My beer is Rheingold the dry beer.**
> **Think of Rheingold whenever you buy beer.**
> **It's not bitter, not sweet,**
> **It's the dry flavored treat.**
> **Won't you try extra dry Rheingold beer?**

Lachlan Beaton: Words of Welcome and Reflections On Wasp

Roy Wilkins: On Rebuilding Spy and the Other Older Boats

Catherine Thacher Barnett: On Spy in the Twenties

The Boats of 1993: Bat, Lotus, Mary Ann, Spy, Tamwock and Wasp

Kearney Kuhlthau: New Words for the Rheingold Song

Thomas Beaton: On Building Ghost, 1992-1994

Introduction of Ghost's crew: John Dickson, Rodney Edwards, Patrick Jurczak, Edward and Beverley Vienckowski

Carla Harkrader: God Bless America

Constance Fortenbaugh: The Christening

Ghost Gets Wet: Anchors Away

Rheingold is available at Central Market and other stores of distinction

The Official Program (fig. 102)

Fig. 103

Prior to the actual launching—getting Ghost's bottom wet—a ceremony involving speech, verse and song was held on the unpaved driveway that passes through the center of Beaton's yard. The pennants decorating Ghost were visible on the eastern side of the drive and a microphone was set up on the western side in the shadow of a shed (fig. 103). Bill opened the program wearing his customary red jacket, a tie that read "Old Overholt," his favorite rye whiskey, and a button that read "Save Princeton Wrestling," his favorite charity (fig. 104). After thanking the folk at Beaton's for the boat they had built and after praising the Rheingold Brewery for the fine beer that was the drink of the day, Bill called upon Kearney Kuhlthau to lead the singing of the Rheingold song. He had already

Fig. 104

Fig. 105

performed in that role at the Last Rivet party in December (see ch. II.4). Now with a much larger crowd, he again took the lead, waving a beer can while singing into the microphone. The volume was overwhelming (fig. 105).

As was appropriate the first dignitary to address the crowd was Lally Beaton (fig. 106). He spoke *qua* senior member of the Beaton clan and past president of David Beaton and Sons. His remarks were characteristically understated. He recounted his own role in securing the survival of the A Cat Class: as president of Beaton's in 1979, he had agreed to build Wasp for Nelson Hartranft and had seen the building through to completion in 1980 (ch. I.1). Most delightful was Lally's account of a telephone conversation that he had had with Nelson prior to the building of Wasp. At the time, Nelson was the owner of Bat, which had broken her mast. Not a poor man, yet not a man of unlimited means, Nelson was concerned about costs and understandably put the question, "How much will a new mast cost?" Lally, never known to overcharge, replied, "One thousand," to which Nelson responded, "I'll take two." And he did take two. One went to Bat; the other would find its place in Wasp.

Roy Wilkins also spoke and did so with inimitable enthusiasm (ch. II.4). He spoke of acquiring Spy in 1978 and having enjoyed sailing her, although her hull was less than tight, so that leaking was a constant problem and pumping mandatory. Then in 1982, what had been a problem almost became a catastrophe. During a race south to Forked River the keel became loose and began to separate from the garboard plank. The situation was so desperate that the boat had to be

Fig. 106

beached and subsequently towed back to Beaton's, where over the next two years Spy got a new keel, ribs and deck frames. As Roy told it, working with Lally and Tom was a life changing experience: it taught him how to slow down and to do things right the first time.

The next speaker had roots in the earliest days of A Cat racing. She was Dood Barnett, the daughter of Frank Thacher, who in the 1920s commissioned the building of Helen and Bat (ch. I.1). Dood was also a neighbor of the Fortenbaughs and had visited Beaton's when Ghost's hull had been painted green (ch. III.1). Now she was eager to attend the launching ceremony, in order to speak on behalf of the Thacher family. It was a windy day, so that Dood was forced to hold onto her hat (fig. 107), but she had no difficulty with words. First she spoke of her father and recounted his involvement in the A Cat Class. From a family point of view, most interesting were her remarks concerning Mr. Thacher's first boat, the Helen. That boat should have been especially dear to him, because he had named the boat after his middle

Fig. 107

daughter. But the boat did not perform well, so Mr. Thacher soon decided that, namesake or not, the Helen had to go. The boat would be replaced by Spy (ch. I.1). In concluding her remarks, Dood addressed Bill, offering well known but still sound advice: "We can't change the wind, but we can adjust the sails." To make sure that the advice would not be forgotten, she presented him with a framed copy of the saying. It may be found today, prominently positioned on the kitchen wall of the Fortenbaugh house in Bay Head.

It was now time to acknowledge that Ghost was about to enter a class that not only had a long history but also was still alive and racing on Barnegat Bay. To that end, Bill introduced the owners of Bat, Lotus, Mary Ann, Spy, Wasp and Tamwock. He presented each with a picture of their boat and in addition took note of the fact that Peter Kellogg was having a new boat, Vapor, built at the Philadelphia Maritime Museum. Not a bashful person and one gifted at seizing the moment, Peter took the microphone and made a bold prediction. He called attention to Ghost's transom, on

Fig. 108

which the boat's name was spelled out in large golden letters (fig. 108). Peter thanked Bill for providing him with such a fine view of Ghost's transom and then added that it would be the last time that he would see the transom. In other words, skippering Vapor, he would finish in front of Ghost, so that Bill and his crew would be looking at Vapor's transom. Humorously provocative, Peter's words brought forth a mixed response from the crowd, but Bill did not take the bait. He played dumb, preferring to let the coming season decide who would have the last laugh (ch. VI.2).

There followed a musical interlude. Kearney Kuhlthau returned to the microphone and offered new words to the familiar Rheingold jingle. These words were preserved in a wooden chest in Bill's basement for eighteen years. Sad to say, in 2012 super storm "Sandy" flooded the basement and in so doing severely damaged all paper documents that were in storage. Weeks later, when volunteers entered the basement with wheelbarrows, they not only removed two feet of sand but also all papers including Kearney's jingle.

Next Bill called on Tom Beaton to speak about his role in organizing and accomplishing the building of Ghost. Tom might have talked at length, detailing the many hours that he and his co-workers had devoted to Ghost: especially the extra hours in the evening during the last weeks immediately preceding the launching. And he might have commented extensively on the craftsmanship required of anyone who would presume to build a boat like Ghost: the selection and cutting of different woods, the fitting together of the many pieces, the preparation of exposed surfaces and their finishing with different oils, varnishes and paints. But never one to boast and preferring few words, Tom told the crowd that he would rather build a boat than deliver a speech. That preference was fully realized in Ghost.

There followed the introduction of Ghost's crew. Recognizing that a well-built boat and an adequate skipper are not sufficient to win races, Bill called forward those present who would be with him on Ghost during the upcoming BBYRA season. They were the talented twosome, Ed and Bev Vienckowski, who were members of the Seaside Park Yacht Club—though Bev had learned to sail in Bay Head (ch. II.4)—Pat Jurczak, who belonged to the Shores Acres Yacht Club, and Rod Edwards and John Dickson, who both learned to sail in Bay Head and remained members there (fig. 109). What Bill actually said in introducing these members of the crew has been forgotten. It is, however, certain that he recognized their talents and what they would contribute on the race course. It is also certain he did not challenge the crew's courage by mentioning the disaster that awaited Ghost thirteen days later (ch. VI.1).

Fig. 109

In concluding this part of the program and before moving on to the launching itself, Bill read two letters, of which the first came from Nelson Hartranft, who is widely regarded as having saved the A Cat class from extinction (ch. I.1) and who was unable to be present on account of business commitments. Hence, Nelson took time to put his thoughts on paper. He described the launching of Ghost as a "truly historic event for the oldest class of racing Barnegat Bay sailboats." He went on to say that it was "absolutely the greatest feeling to know (that) so many people have come to love these boats as much as I do." Finally he focused on Beaton's, mentioned Tom, Russ and Paul by name, and extended his best wishes "for building such a fine craft."

The second letter was from Walter Smedley, who hailed from suburban Philadelphia and like so many Philadelphians spent many summers in Beach Haven, where he was a member of the Little Egg Harbor Yacht Club and served as commodore in 1967. He also had many friends in Bay Head including Bill. Both had gone to the Haverford School on the Philadelphia Main Line and both had shared good times in Beach Haven, when Bill went south to race Sneakboxes, M Scows and E Scows at the LEHYC. Learning that Ghost was to be launched on June twelfth and being unable to attend the ceremony, he put pen to paper and saluted the "momentous occasion" with four lines of verse:

Here's to Ghost, on the twelfth of June,
may she have the most, and none too soon,
Of perfect starts, and joyous crew,
And win after win her whole life through!

What a wonderful wish: well crafted and one that may be called prescient, at least in regard to Ghost's first seven years.

The program concluded on a high note. Carla Harkrader took the microphone and did a Kate Smith look alike/sing alike. She belted out "God Bless America", putting body and soul into a rendition that was every bit the equal of Smith's performances before the home games of the Philadelphia Flyers. It was widely believed that when Kate sang, the Flyers won. Now that Carla had sung, it was rumored on the Bay that Ghost would win in '94.

3. The Christening

After speech, verse and song, it was time for Ghost to be christened. It would not be baptism by total immersion—that would occur thirteen days later during the first race (ch. VI.1)—rather it would be a nautical ritual: the breaking of a bottle on the bow of Ghost. There had been talk of the very best champagne, but that was deemed not only too expensive and but also inappropriate. More suitable would be a bottle of Rheingold, and a quart bottle, not 12 but 32 ounces—a veritable magnum—yet still inexpensive.

In preparation for the ritual, Ghost was lifted off its supports by the travel lift. In fig. 110, we see Russ and Connie, Bill's wife, watching the procedure closely. Connie will be performing the baptism and toward that end she is carrying on her hip a bottle of Rheingold. It has been carefully wrapped to guard against flying glass, when the bottle shattered.

As soon as Ghost had been elevated to a proper height, Tom began removing the metal jacks that had supported Ghost, while Russ attached lines to the stern. They would be used later to secure the stern, once the boat had been lowered into the water (fig. 111).

Next Ghost was moved backwards, stern first, until the boat was suspended over the water, but with her bow close to the launching pad. That would permit Connie to perform the baptism (fig. 112).

Fig. 110

Fig. 111

When Ghost was properly positioned, Connie approached Ghost. In her hand was the baptismal quart of Rheingold (fig 113). Her eyes were closed, perhaps in prayer to Poseidon, god of the sea. Then with eyes open, she cried aloud, "In the name of mothers and daughters, fathers and sons, I now christen you Ghost," and struck the bow.

Fig. 112

Fig. 113

Fig. 114

Fig. 115

Strike she did, but to the delight of the onlookers, the bottled failed to break. To the right in fig. 114, we see Mark Dawson, who did much to put Ghost together (see ch.V.1 fig. 100 and ch.VI. figs. 118 and 119). He is laughing aloud. The same can be said of Pat Jurczak's daughter, who is next to Mark. On the left is Peter Fortenbaugh, the son of Connie and Bill, who seems respectfully amused.

Connie regained her composure, tried again and succeeded in producing an explosion of Rheingold beer (fig. 115). That brought joy to all.

As Ghost was lowered into the water, the band struck up "Anchors Away". The descent was flawless and once in the water—to no one's surprise—Ghost floated according to the design of Francis Sweisguth: water met the waterline. The craftsmen at Beaton's had built to perfection (fig. 116).

Fig. 116

VI
SEVEN TIMES BAY CHAMPION

1. 1994 Disaster Followed by Recovery

After the memorable launching, Ghost needed to be finished. There were still thirteen days before the first race of the BBYRA season. That would be June twenty-fifth, so that completion seemed quite possible. The stub mast needed to be replaced with the real mast, which had been largely completed before the launching and stored in the rigging shed. There completion occurred, after which replacement would be accomplished.

In fig. 117, Ghost has been moved from the launching area to the rigging dock, where she is tied up in the vicinity of the rigging ladder. In addition, Ghost's mast has been brought onto the dock and placed on horses, in such a way that it is partially under the rigging ladder. There it will be lifted off the supports, shifted from horizontal to vertical and lowered into Ghost.

Fig. 117

Now in fig. 118, Ghost's mast has been lifted up, so that Michael Delorme and Mike Dawson (left and right respectively) are able to guide the mast's butt into position, first through the king plank on the deck and then into a rectangular slot below the deck (IV.2). To the right and on the dock, Russ Manheimer is seen at the foot of the rigging ladder. In that position he can observe the progress being made on the deck of Ghost and lower the mast when it is time to do so. Once the mast has been lowered and fitted into its slot below, chocks will be inserted on the deck between the mast and the king plank. In addition wire stays will be secured to straps, often called chainplates, which appear above deck on both sides next to the toe rail. Once that is accomplished, the mast will be secure at deck level.

Fig. 118

In fig. 119, the mast is in place above and below the deck. Michael Delorme and Mike Dawson are still at work on the foredeck, having begun the process of attaching the stays. Tom Beaton can be seen on the wooden walkway, making sure that Ghost is adequately tied.

Fig. 119

After the work of securing the mast had been completed, a member of the yard crew climbed the rigging ladder to inspect not only the stays and halyard high up on the mast but also the masthead fly—the sailor's weathervane or cock—which is attached to the very top of the mast (fig. 120). Typically the fly is held in place by three short screws, which can come loose if the fly is knocked. That may be unlikely during the raising of a mast, but it can happen. Indeed, it is typical of Beaton's fine workmanship to make a final inspection, where others might not do so.

Once the mast was in place, the boom was attached to the mast along with the pulleys that would be needed to trim the sail. The deck was still without cleats for the

Fig. 120

halyards and for the backstays. There was a cleat forward for the painter or towline but no fixtures aft for stern lines. All these items belong to a finished boat and would be ready in time for the first race. Other details like the cabin doors would not be in place. They could be used for an overnight aboard Ghost—keeping mosquitoes away—or for closing up the cabin securely, should Ghost be unattended for a long period of time (see ch. II.7). But for racing the doors were useless and even an impediment, should equipment within the cabin suddenly be needed. Such considerations encouraged the crew to prepare to enter the first race, and the shop-crew at Beaton's was happy to cooperate. In thirteen days much could be accomplished, and indeed it was.

On Friday afternoon, June twenty-fourth, the day before the first race, four members of the team—Bill, Ed, Pat and John (ch. V.2)—came together at Beaton's, intending to go for a practice sail. Ghost was afloat at dock and appeared inviting. The sail was already on the spars, and the mainsheet was in place, running from the end of the boom to the traveler, back to the boom, down again to the traveler and so on (fig. 121). To be sure, the shop crew was still at work on details. In particular, Russ and Tom were busy attaching fixtures to the deck, but that would take little time. In the photo, Pat is seen waiting patiently with hands on hips. The person leaning over the boom watching Russ and Tom is most likely Bill. If that is correct, he might have spent his time better reflecting on what needed to be accomplished for the boat to be adequately prepared for racing. To be sure, the mainsheet is visible with its many pulleys creating significant mechanical advantage, but should the wind be heavy and should there be no foot braces for the trimmer, even the strongest of trimmers would find it all but impossible to trim the huge sail that is the mark of an A Cat. And that would be the case on Saturday.

Fig. 121

Looking forward to the first race, Ghost's crew was eager to get started but also less than clear headed. How could they not have seen that there were no seats and no foot braces? Remarkably on Friday that seemed unimportant, for the wind was light, no more than a gentle breeze. The crew was able to sail either sitting on the floor-boards, or on the deck, or standing up. For those who spent their youth racing, e.g., Sneakboxes, G Sloops and Comets, a lack of seats and foot braces will have seemed quite normal, but those boats have a mainsail that is small, not to be compared with that of an A Cat, whose crew normally number seven or eight. The fact that on Friday

Ghost's crew numbered no more than four, should have raised a red flag. For an A Cat to be manageable with only four persons aboard, the wind must be light, no more than a gentle breeze. On the Friday in question, the wind was indeed light, and the crew, happy to be out on the water, failed to remember that a strong southerly is typical of a June afternoon. Had just one member of the crew reflected on the time of year and what one should expect, he might have asked, whether it would be possible to race Ghost in her present condition. Should the southerly come in and top fifteen, even eighteen, miles per hour, disaster was a serious possibility. It is fair to say that the crew exhibited recklessness—or better, stupidity—in the extreme.

When Saturday came, the wind was light in the morning and only moderate when Ghost left Beaton's under tow. In fig 122, the woodshop at Beaton's and the sail loft above the shop can be seen in the distance to the left of Ghost. Pat Jurczak is on the foredeck of Ghost. He is untying the painter or bowline, in order that the thicker, stronger towline can take over. In fig. 123 Ghost has shed the painter in favor of a proper towline. The sail appears fat because it is catching wind, both the southerly which is still moderate and that created by being towed into the wind. Bill is seen standing and looking ahead. He apparently failed to recognize the troubles that awaited Ghost as the wind increased.

Fig. 122

Fig. 123

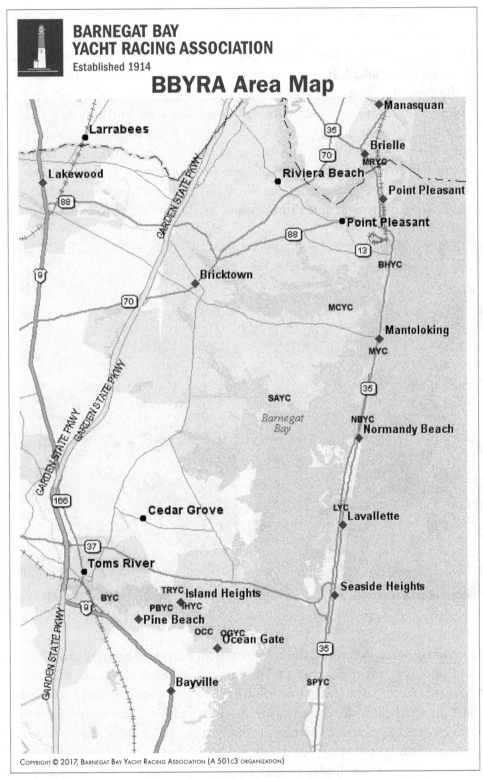

Fig. 124

While Ghost was still under tow, heading toward the up-bay race course south of Shore Acres, and west of Normandy Beach and Lavallette (see fig. 124 Map with the Appendix to ch. VI.1), the wind began building and the crew responded appropriately by reefing the sail. It was a small reef, but it seemed adequate. Indeed, at the start of the race, the wind was still manageable, so that during the first upwind leg, Ghost moved through the water with ease, showing a decent bow-wave and good speed (fig. 125). It may have been an exhilarating moment, but it soon would be otherwise. The wind continued to increase, so that on the second upwind leg Ghost became difficult to control (fig. 126). Bill was no longer able to steer: he lost control while sliding across the boat, under the tiller, and ending up in the leeward bilge. He called on Ed, much stronger and a fine skipper in his own right, to take over the helm.

Fig. 125   Fig. 126

The change at the helm and the tenacity of all on board bought time, but Aeolus, the Wind god, was not to be denied. He decided to teach the crew a lesson and to do so in a special manner. Instead of rolling Ghost over with a single strong blast, so that the hull was perpendicular to the water—the sail laid flat across the water and unable to be lifted as the boat swamped—the god chose to sink Ghost before the hull was perpendicular to the water. To do so was a simple matter of physics. An A Cat is a heavy boat, which must displace water equivalent to circa 4,500 pounds. When she fails to do so, she sinks. That point comes before a vertical tip-over, and in the case of Ghost it was reached, while the boat still seemed capable of moving forward. That was a mistaken impression. Suddenly the hull began to slide into the water, ever deeper, so that water rushed over the coaming into Ghost's wide cockpit.

In fig. 127, Ghost's hull has all but disappeared under water. Her sail can be seen still floating on top of the water, but there is no way to reverse the situation without outside intervention. The large motorboat nearby appears to be an official boat. If so, it will have used its radio to summon a smaller boat that would be able to maneuver close to Ghost. It could help the crew bring the sail down the mast, so that the hull of Ghost might be brought to an upright position and taken under tow to calmer water.

Fig. 127

In fig. 128 we see Ghost under tow with a float in the shape of a ball attached to the top of the mast. One of the two boats seen in front of Ghost is likely to have passed the float to a member of Ghost's crew, who attached it to the top of the mast in order to prevent the mast from going under water and getting stuck in the mud. That might have done serious harm to Ghost's sail, and it would have made it quite difficult to right the boat for towing.

Fig. 128 also tells us that the crew of Ghost was unable to get the sail completely down while the boat was still on its side. Nevertheless, the sail is far enough down, so that the boat could be righted and towed out of the open bay with its rolling waves into the calmer waters north of Hankins Point. There the boat was pumped out (fig. 129) and ultimately towed back to Beaton's. The rescue operation will have lasted well over an hour.

Fig. 128

Fig. 129

That was a disastrous beginning, which would soon be memorialized in song by two local wordsmiths: Bob Post and George Lucas, who took their cue from the "Great Ship Titanic."

Oh they built the sailboat Ghost to sail the open Bay
And they thought they had a ship that would never lose her way;
But with God's almighty blow
Up and over she did go.
It was sad when the great Ghost went down;
It was sad, so sad;
It was sad, so sad;
It was sad when the great Ghost went down
To the bottom of the Bay.
Skipper and crew had more than they could do.
It was sad when the great Ghost went down.

Fig. 130

Sad it was, but there were others within the sailing community who were dismissive. That did not escape Ed, who wrote, "Based on the reaction from others to that (Ghost's) first day performance, it became apparent that Ghost was not being considered all that serious(ly) as a contender. (Wrong!) Any such thinking was misguided" (*A Cats* p. 107). To be sure, the crew of Ghost was deflated—seriously so—but not about to quit. Over the next six days the shop crew at Beaton's was able to make necessary improvements: most important, seats and foot-braces were installed. Equally important was an addition to the crew: namely, Rich Miller, whom Ed knew from the Seaside Park Yacht Club. Invited to come aboard by Ed, Rich accepted, bringing to the boat much needed weight for strong winds. See fig.130, in which Rich is seated beside Bill. The difference is size is obvious. A Cats often sail with a crew of eight and in heavy wind at least one 200 plus pounder is all but necessary. Whether Rich topped 240 is unknown, but given his size he found his place immediately behind the back stay, which is affixed to the deck roughly midway between bow and stern. That kept the boat balanced fore and aft and most importantly allowed Rich to place himself at the widest part of the boat: maximum leverage against heavy blasts of wind. Lest there be a misunderstanding, it should be added with emphasis that Rich was anything but mindless ballast. He was a good sailor, who knew on his own when he needed to be in the cockpit and when he was wanted on the windward deck, facing outwards with legs overboard. In addition, he knew how to reef Ghost's sail while underway and when to loosen and tighten the outhaul and downhaul as conditions changed. Clearly Rich's coming aboard was a transforming moment. Indeed, the value of his presence was made clear straightway in the second race of the season.

That race was on the lower bay, hosted by the Island Heights Yacht Club. The start was on the northern side of the course near the Mathis Bridge, which joins the mainland to the peninsula (see fig. 124). No longer overpowered by wind, Ghost showed what she could do. Instead of approaching the starting line on starboard tack as the rest of the fleet did, Ghost approached the line on port tack, came about under the fleet, trimmed in the sail and got off the line unimpeded and at full speed. Ghost quickly had the lead and would never lose it. Ghost kept pulling away, so that after rounding the weather mark and heading downwind, the crew could enjoy the sight behind. The rest of the fleet was not close and throughout the downwind leg fell further back. Why is something of a mystery, except that over the summer Ghost would prove herself fast downwind in all conditions: both heavy and light wind, rough and smooth water. Whatever the true explanation might be, Ghost continued to lead the fleet throughout the second race and finished well ahead.

The next Saturday brought the third race of the season. It was sailed on the up-bay course and hosted by the Mantoloking and Manasquan River Yacht Clubs. The crew of Ghost was eager to establish itself as a winning team and did so by finishing unchallenged in first place. After that the wind failed to cooperate, so that the fourth race of the season had to be abandoned due to insufficient wind, and the fifth race was canceled on account of excessive wind. Racing resumed with the sixth race, which was hosted by the Ocean Gate and Pine Beach Yacht Clubs. Ghost continued her winning ways. The seventh race was exceptional in that Ghost was a no-show and with good reason. During the week prior to the race, the skipper had a growing cyst removed from his neck. But neither he nor the crew would be slowed up by a single absence. Indeed, Ghost went on to win the last three races of the season.

Certainly good sailing—e.g., aggressive starts, covering boats on upwind legs, maintaining a proper heel to windward when running downwind—played a major role in Ghost's success, but it would be a mistake to think that good sailing by itself was sufficient to ensure continued success. Also important was mid-week maintenance. The boat was kept dry—sponge dry—in order to prevent Ghost from soaking up water and thereby putting on weight. Perhaps most important was the time spent maintaining a fast bottom. The bottom was covered with antifouling paint, which could never be as fast as hard racing paint. But weekly sanding and cleaning the topsides with soap can make a significant difference, and it did. Here the Ghost crew is indebted to Teddy Beaton, Lally's brother and Tom's uncle, who was in charge of the yard and made sure that Ghost could be hauled on Friday afternoon for sanding and scrubbing before the Saturday race. Certainly Teddy was generous with his time, but he and the bookkeepers were also generous in that during this first year the haul occurred without cost. That changed the next year and rightly so. In the future Ghost would be hauled less often.

It is tempting to say no more concerning Ghost's first season: the initial sinking followed by a string of wins and the importance of a clean bottom might be deemed sufficient. But there is more: a classic tip-over occurred in August, and a day of drifting followed in September. The tip-over occurred during a special Sunday race hosted by the Island Heights Yacht club. The prize was one of the oldest and most revered of all the A Cat trophies. It was first sailed for in 1922 and carried the name Rodman Wanamaker Yacht Trophy. Appropriately the race would be sailed on that portion of the lower bay known as the Wanamaker course. Ghost was entered and the crew was willing, at least for the most part. It was Sunday after a long Saturday on the water, and one member of the crew dropped out. He was replaced by Vita Cox. Moreover, being a good family man Ed had brought along his two young boys: Alex and Tim. Fair enough, but this particular Sunday not only was the wind blowing over fifteen knots but also the bay was covered with rolling waves, so that stumbling within the boat seemed likely and even dangerous. An immediate worry was Ed's young boys, who might get hurt should someone bump into them or even fall on top of them. After only brief discussion, it was decided that they would be out of harm's way, were they below in the cabin. That seemed sensible but would be proven foolish.

The initial windward leg went well, but as Ghost approached the leeward mark on port tack, it became clear that were Ghost to proceed upwind on an advantageous course, it was imperative to jibe immediately at the mark onto starboard tack. Ghost did jibe, but Bill's aging muscles were unable to control the tiller and to steady the boat on her upwind course. The boat quickly rolled on to her side, the hull became perpendicular to the water, and the cockpit began to take in water, which would soon fill the cabin. At this point Vita exhibited extraordinary presence of mind. She remembered the boys and crouching down entered the cabin, choosing the side that was all but submerged. Had she not acted so quickly and so correctly, one of the boys would have been underwater and perhaps unable to find his way out. The rest of the story hardly needs telling. Ghost's crew spent a full hour struggling to get the sail down, right the boat and bail it out with buckets and pump. That was less than pleasant, but four lessons were learned.

First and most important, when wind and sea are intense, it's a bad idea to go below. That is especially true when the person below is young and inexperienced. Second, when jibing in light to medium air, the centerboard should be down to facilitate steering. The boat needs sideward resistance in order to turn well. But in a blow it is not a good idea to jibe with full board down. Turning will involve a loss of forward momentum but not diminish the pressure that the wind is putting on the boat. Less board will make it possible for the boat to slide ever so little sideways and thereby avoid tripping over the board, i.e. rolling over and filling with water (see Appendix to ch. VIII.1 on fig. 157). Third, when jibing in heavy air, the skipper should begin turning the boat back as soon as the boom begins to change sides. And fourth, sometimes it is better not to count on the skipper's strength. Rather, sail beyond the mark and come about. A Cats are not as fast as E Scows. If the move is properly made, little distance will be lost. Moreover, if a competitor jibes poorly so that his boat teeters on its side before settling down, distance may not be lost. Indeed, it may be gained.

Finally there was a day of drifting. Ghost had already experienced that in July when what should have been the fourth race of the BBYRA season was abandoned by the regatta committee. Later in September when the season was over, the Island Heights Yacht Club hosted what was and still is humorously referred to as the "A Cat Worlds". Despite her name, Ghost does not "ghost along" when wind speed becomes immeasurable, nor does Ghost's skipper work magic at the helm. Ghost did not finish last, but her showing was uncharacteristically poor. Nevertheless, an overcast sky and flat water produced some charming, even romantic photos, two of which are reproduced on the immediately following pages.

In fig. 131, Ghost has been towed from the Island Heights Yacht Club to the Wanamaker course, where the Worlds are to be sailed. Ed is on the foredeck pulling up the sail, and Rich is bent over bringing in the halyard. The sail is not luffing, the water shows only the slightest sign of wind, and the overcast sky suggests that the wind may not strengthen. Hoisting the sail seems hasty, but the crew of Ghost may feel obliged to hoist the sail and cast off, in order that the boat in front can do the same. Or is the crew of Ghost being foolishly optimistic?

In fig. 132, Ghost is on a slight heel, not because the wind has strengthened, but because the crew is sitting to leeward. A minimal wake can be detected to leeward and behind the hull. Apparently Ghost's tall mast is catching some wind, but not much: enough to move forward gently, but too little for optimal racing. Nevertheless, the picture has a certain charm. The white sail stands out against the darkened sky, and the water reflects the white of the sail. Laureen Vellante, who took the photo, had an eye for the romantic.

Fig. 131

Fig. 132

Appendix to ch. VI.1
The BBYRA Race Courses

The Map printed above as fig. 124 carries the heading "BBYRA Area Map." It has been reproduced with the permission of the Barnegat Bay Yacht Racing Association. Toward the top of the map, the letters BHYC locate the Bay Head Yacht Club at the northern most point of the Bay. Other clubs are also located by abbreviations in upper case letters. E.g. MCYC places the Metedeconk River Yacht Club southwest of the BHYC on the south side of the Metedeconk River. Today that river serves as a race course for both the BHYC and MCYC. As late as the 1960s it was used for part of the BBYRA summer series (the morning races of the first weekend). But today it plays no role in the BBYRA summer series. Rather, the summer series of the BBYRA takes place in two areas further south. There is the upper bay course, which is north of the Seaside Heights bridge, known as the Mathis Bridge, and the lower bay course which is south of the bridge. The former is commonly referred to as the "Green Island Course" and is located between Hankins Island to the east and Green Island to the west. Or on the BBYRA Area Map, it may be placed west of the NBYC and the LYC. In contrast, the lower bay course has no single name and may be spoken of as two distinct courses. There is the "Wanamaker Course" located between Good Luck Point to the southeast and Wanamaker Park to the northwest, where Tom's River opens up and becomes part of the Bay. In addition, there is the "Seaside Park Course", which is located to the west of the Seaside Park Yacht Club. Nevertheless, the distinction is often blurred, for fast boats like E Scows and boats none too slow like A Cats are frequently given courses that extend over both the Wanamaker and Seaside Courses.

2. 1995–1998 Ghost Wins but is Challenged

After the Worlds as autumn progressed and the temperature began to drop, Ghost was taken out of water at Beaton's and stored for the winter in a large shed south of the launching area. There the boat sat on blocks above a dirt floor. The roof of the shed kept rain and snow out of the boat, while the dirt floor held moisture, which prevented Ghost from drying out excessively during the spring as warm weather began to return. In early June, Ghost was removed from the shed, her bottom painted and the bright work given a new coat of varnish. Not inexpensive maintenance, but well worthwhile. A beautiful boat should be kept that way, and a fast bottom called for sanding and fresh paint. In addition the rigging was inspected and worn lines replaced. In sum, every effort was made to ensure Ghost's success in 1995.

In fig. 133, Ghost has been removed from the winter storage shed and placed on cradle-like supports in front of the paint shop (white doors), where she will be worked on. The deadwood appears to have been sanded, which is true, but the sanding occurred during the previous summer on Fridays in preparation for Saturday races. The deadwood will be sanded once again and then painted with a light gray anti-fouling paint. The difference in color between bottom and rudder—the replacement rudder made during the previous season (ch. II.6. 2)—is attributable to a

Fig. 133

difference in paint. That on the rudder has greater anti-fouling properties, because the rudder is not under the boat but sticks out to the rear. There it catches sun light, which promotes fouling. That prompted a change in paint already during the first season. The change would not be the last, as the search for a better/faster antifouling paint would continue over the years ahead.

Taken as a whole, the summer of 1995 was indeed a successful season: Ghost won the BBYRA championship, but the boat was not as dominant as she had been the year before. She won three races, finished second once and third three times. That accounts for eight races out of the scheduled ten. One race was canceled and another was cut by the entire fleet in order that boats might sail in August at the annual Invitational Regatta sponsored by the Little Egg Harbor Yacht Club on the waters west of Beach Haven. Ghost won the regatta (see ch. VII.2). Ghost also returned to Island Heights to compete for the Wanamaker Trophy and this time went home a winner. The same is true of the Worlds. Clearly the crew of Ghost had done well in special races, but in the seasons ahead it would pick and choose. Devoting Sundays as well as Saturdays to racing Ghost was time consuming. Special races were for the most part sailed Sunday afternoons on the lower bay, which meant long tows back to Bay Head, often arriving late for dinner. And Monday was a workday.

Before leaving 1995, it should be noted that Peter Kellogg's new boat, Vapor (see ch. I.2), which had failed to distinguish herself in 1994, was doing better. Vapor won two races, finished second twice, third twice as well as fourth and sixth once each. She finished the season behind Ghost in second place. That awakened the Ghost crew; going forward, Vapor was not to be ignored. The boat had speed, but what caught Bill's eye early in the season was a change in rigging. The wire in Vapor's backstays had been removed in favor of spectra, a much lighter material that would reduce weight aloft. Bill phoned the builder John Brady to convey a gentle protest. John acknowledged the change but saw no reason to return to wire. After all, improvements were part of the evolution of the A Cat from its inception. That is, of course, true. The naval architect Charles Mower, who designed the first A Cat, Mary Ann, introduced changes in his second boat, Bat, and did so unannounced (see ch. I.1). Accordingly, Bill protested no further. But he also saw in spectra the intensification of a worrisome trend—what some folk have called an "arms race"—which would be difficult to control and inevitably would drive up costs. Sailors of modest means would steer clear of the class.

In 1996 Rod Edwards retired from Ghost. For two seasons he had not only crewed on Ghost but also used his own motorboat to tow Ghost to regattas including that sailed on the waters of Little Egg Harbor, some forty miles south of Bay Head. Rod never requested contributions to cover the cost of gas, and always got Ghost to the race course in a timely manner. Generous and reliable, he would be sorely missed, but his departure was understandable. He was approaching seventy and feeling his age. Happily John Dickson was prepared to take over towing duties, using his own boat, and Jim Cadranell replaced Rod as a regular member of the crew. Jim was a native of Seattle, Washington, and had grown up racing in deep water and light air. Racing in the comparatively shallow water of Barnegat Bay, when the southerly wind blew hard, was a new experience, which Jim embraced and mastered.

The beginning of the 1996 BBYRA season saw Ghost on top, winning the first two races. After that came two seconds, a first and third. Two races were canceled by the committee and Ghost went to Little Egg where it finished second (see ch. VII.2). Taken together these finishes were nothing to be ashamed of, but they also put Ghost in a tie for the bay championship. Vapor's finishes were three firsts, two seconds and a sixth. On a low point scoring system that allowed each boat one drop or throw out, Ghost and Vapor were tied: the former dropped a third and the latter a sixth. The last race would decide the championship. The Ghost's crew did little to prepare. In fact, Bill was preoccupied with German friends from the University of Saarbrücken. There was the occasional joke—Ghost will "vaporize" Vapor—but little else. In contrast, Vapor had let go most of its crew in order to bring on board a truly talented and tested foursome: Willie De Camp, Jon Wright, Doug Love and Dick Wight. Add in Peter Wright who was already a member of the Vapor crew, and it was clear that Peter Kellogg was taking the race with exceptional seriousness. He wanted the championship for Vapor, and he might have had it.

Between the preparatory gun and the start, Bill's thoughts had wandered, so that Ed had to tell him that he was far from the starting line and had better come about straightway. Bill did that and at the gun was on starboard tack, a length or two behind Vapor. He assessed the situation and immediately tacked onto port, heading south in anticipation of a southerly shift in the wind, which was still building. Vapor chose not to cover. That choice remains a mystery. Perhaps there was too much talent aboard, which led to discussion and failure to respond in a timely manner—a landlubber might say "Too many cooks spoil the broth"—but whatever the explanation, Ghost had broken free, continued south toward the lay line, tacked on a southerly shift and crossed in front of Vapor on the way to the first mark. At the mark Mary Ann rounded first, always fast upwind but not in competition for the championship. Ghost chose to let Mary Ann go and to concentrate on Vapor. On a subsequent downwind leg, Ed suggested blanketing Mary Ann with a view to overtaking her, but Bill chose to leave Mary Ann alone and to stay with Vapor.

Fig. 134

In fig. 134, we see Ghost running downwind, following Mary Ann but not taking her wind. Ghost's concern is Vapor, which is behind Ghost and will remain there, close enough to see Ghost's transom (see ch.V.2) but unable to catch up, let alone pass. Bill is steering, Ed is on the sheet and Bev is on the boom. Rich is easily identified on the left, and John is on the right able to assist Ed with trimming, if necessary.

The decision to stay with Vapor proved decisive. Mary Ann won not only the last race of the summer series but also the Sewell Cup, which was traditionally awarded to the winner of the last race. Ghost gave the crew of Mary Ann a hearty salute of congratulations, crossed the finish line close behind in second place and won the series championship. Vapor finished third in silence. The disappointment among so many talented sailors was patent.

The next two seasons Ghost was not seriously challenged for the bay championship. In 1997 she won seven races and finished fourth once. One race was canceled and another cut in order that the fleet might go to Little Egg. On the low point scoring system, the fourth was dropped, so that Ghost finished the BBYRA season with a perfect score. In 1998 Ghost was not perfect but clearly on top of the fleet. She had five firsts, one second and two thirds. One race was canceled and one was cut for Little Egg. Vapor slipped back to fourth in 1997 and then improved to third in 1998. In both years Wasp finished second. It is fair to say that being challenged in 1996 had awakened the crew of Ghost. Both in 1997 and again in 1998, the championship was won by seven points, and both times the crew saw fit to enjoy the awards ceremony.

Fig. 135

Following tradition, the ceremony was held after the last race of the season on the front porch of the Seaside Park Yacht Club. In fig. 135, the porch is pictured. It faces the Bay and happily has not been enclosed for upscale diners, who demand air conditioning. That makes the building a grand site for the annual BBYRA awards ceremony. Officers in uniform take over the lower porch—it is well above ground level—and the recipients of awards mount the stairs to receive their prizes and then descend the stairs to the applause of sailors and friends of sailing who fill the patio below.

Fig. 136

In a photo dated to 1997 fig. 136, we see Ghost's crew celebrating its victory. Rod Edwards—he always returned for the prize ceremony—is leading the crew in singing the Rheingold song. The three ladies of Ghost—left to right, Bev Vienckowski, Jeannie Kellington, and Ellyn Shannon—can be seen waiving Rheingold flags. A fourth person waving a Rheingold flag is obscured behind Bill, who is holding a bottle of Rheingold. Notice the red band on the neck of a brown bottle. Seen to the right alongside Rod, is Rich, He must be confused; his bottle has a yellow band on green glass. That's not Rheingold.

After singing the Rheingold song, the crew of Ghost descended the stairs. The ladies led the way with their Rheingold flags. The men followed. In fig. 137, we see Rich, Jim and Bill, who is carrying not only the championship pennant but also the Sewell cup.

Three weeks after the close of the 1998 season, the crew of Ghost came together for a festive occasion. This time the crew was joined by family and most importantly by the people who built Ghost and maintained her over five years. Tom, Paul and Russ were present, as were both Mark, whose sails had been tested and proven to be winners, and Teddy, who made sure that Ghost would be lifted out of the water on Fridays for cleaning, at first every Friday and then biweekly. The invitation to the gathering—with the cheerful ghost—is reproduced in fig. 138.

Fig. 137

Hurrah for Ghost

A Quinquennial Celebration

Recalling five years of racing
on Barnegat Bay
Ghost
invites you to a dinner
at the Bay Head Yacht Club
on Sunday September 27

bar at six, dinner at seven

rsvp: 899-2771

Think of Rheingold whenever you buy beer

Fig. 138

3. 1999–2000 New Hands on the Tiller

For five consecutive years Bill had been at the helm of Ghost. His ability to focus—one might say his intensity—while racing was clear to all who were aboard. The same is true of his capacity for having fun, once the finish line had been crossed. One might have expected Bill to stay at the helm and to try for a sixth Bay Championship, but that was not to be. Instead academic work took precedence. Bill was committed to being in Italy at a research center during the late spring and early summer of 1999, after which he would visit the Vatican Library and spend most of the summer in Germany working on the scientific works of Theophrastus. Put differently, he would not be wearing his familiar red lifejacket and tie-on cap, while steering Ghost around the buoys. He needed to find a replacement. That person was not hard to find. Indeed, the choice was obvious: namely, Ed. He had been working the mainsheet on Ghost for five years and had an excellent sense of what Ghost could and could not do. Accordingly, Bill asked Ed whether he would like to skipper Ghost throughout the BBYRA season. Ed did not hesitate. He accepted and set about finding his own replacement: someone who not only had the strength to trim the sail in a blow but also understood sailboat racing. That meant someone who without prompting could be expected to trim and ease the sail in response to changes in the velocity and direction of the wind. And equally important, it meant finding someone who could offer tactical advice that would be trustworthy. Ed chose Russell Lucas.

Bill returned from Europe prior to the last race and was understandably eager to join the crew. Since it was clear that Ghost would win the championship—with six first place finishes, one second and a throw out the championship was locked up—Bill did not hesitate to ask Ed whether he might join the crew but not up front on the foredeck. That would entail running around the mast on each tack, which would be precarious were the wind strong and the waves high. Ed agreed and Bill was able to observe the team in action from a position toward the rear of the boat and forward of Russell. It was soon obvious that the team was working well together and that Ed rivaled Bill in intensity. In front on the next to last leg, a reach before a short tack to the finish line, Ed kept the pressure on, urging Russell to trim and ease the sail according to the wind. What Ed was saying made excellent sense, but Russell felt the pressure and uttered a single expression of displeasure. It was a wonderfully human moment, which reminded Bill of his own intensity. Moreover, Ghost soon arrived at the finish line a winner. Everyone was all smiles and ready for a Rheingold moment.

That moment came quickly. Ed sailed to a mooring where Ghost was tied up. The sail came down, the Rheingold flag was hoisted and the crew went ashore. In fig. 139 Ghost is at anchor and the crew ashore. The flag is not at full mast. That may reflect

Fig. 139

haste to get ashore, but when the wind is up or likely to come up, not hoisting the flag to the top of the mast seems prudent, or is it overly cautious?

Whether haste or caution, beers were soon opened all around, so that the Ghost crew was in a jolly mood when it was the time for the awards ceremony. The ascent to the porch of the Yacht Club was accomplished without a single stumble. Bill addressed the crowd in German, congratulating Ed and praising Rheingold beer (Rheingold is as good a German name as there is). Ed spoke next in his best French, after which he received the traditional Bay championship pennant and the Sewell Cup as well. The crew on the porch and spectators below sang together the Rheingold song and did so with great enthusiasm: a delightful conclusion to a successful campaign.

Fig. 140

In fig. 140 we see the jolly crew posing for a photo after the awards ceremony. From left to right we see Bev, Jeannie Kellington, Rich, Ed who is proudly holding the Sewell cup, Jim, Bill, Deezi Lindenmayer, Kim the Blond Bombshell and Ellyn. Winning is always a joyful moment, but the Ghost crew had very few down moments even in defeat. The secret: Rheingold is a guaranteed mood enhancer. During the following winter, Bill was concerned how best to move forward. His summer abroad had worked a bipartite effect on him. He realized that he enjoyed sailing and wanted to continue, but he also realized that Greek philosophy was even more important to him. Add in a strong sense of advancing years, and Bill decided to invite onto Ghost someone who could share time on the tiller during the 2000 season. That person was Dan Crabbe (see ch. I.1 Appendix 1), who accepted the invitation and would remain involved with Ghost for eighty years. Dan brought Ghost a fine hand on the tiller and expert knowledge of the lower Bay: the Wanamaker course and the waters off Seaside Park. But there is more. He also contributed a fourth Battle Flag: one that pictures Ghost holding a bottle of Rheingold in his left hand. As depicted Ghost lacks a right hand (artistic license). In fig. 141, we see Bill on the left and Dan on the right holding up Dan's flag. The photo was not made in the year 2000, when Dan joined the crew of Ghost. Indeed, it was taken on July 10, 2016, the day that Bill became an octogenarian. Dan is not far behind in years; the happy smile befits Dan's unfailing good humor.

Fig. 141

Bill and Dan worked well together. They won the Bay championship in the year 2000 with seven firsts and two seconds. Those finishes converted to a perfect season, for the officers of the Bay had adopted a new scoring system that permitted two throw outs. The seconds were dropped and Ghost ended up with all firsts.

As usual the last race was sailed at Seaside and the winner would take home the Sewell Cup. The winner was Ghost, so that the BBYRA season should have ended with a rousing rendition of the Rheingold song. But that was not to be. A member of the Toms River Yacht Club had written to the BBYRA protesting the singing of a song that focused on a particularly popular brand of beer. That was alleged to be out of place, not because sailors do not drink beer—especially Rheingold, which was distributed locally by the Point Pleasant Distributors, owned and operated by the Wardell family—but because there would be present at the awards ceremony persons who were not yet twenty-one, the legal drinking age in New Jersey. What silliness! The officers of the BBYRA might have repelled the protester with two words, "Lighten up." Or they might have exhibited sophistication, pointing out that singing the Rheingold song actually elevates the awards program. For the lyrics are sung to the tune of Emil Waldteufel's "Estudiantina Valse" (The Students' Waltz, composed in 1883). Instead, the officers caved, and Bill was told before the awards ceremony that the Rheingold song should not be sung. Nobody told that to the spectators, and when the crew of Ghost began to leave the porch in silence, there was a ground swell of support from the patio below. The spectators without prompting sang the Rheingold song, while one member of the Toms River Yacht Club—not the writer of the disapproving letter—waltzed about in perfect three quarter time, all the while holding high a Rheingold umbrella. That heartened the Ghost team, so that the long tow back to Bay Head was a joyful one. Indeed, the original Rheingold flag, now seven years old, was flying from the top of Ghost's mast (fig. 142), and Bill was able to reflect on a fifty year anniversary. He had won his first BBYRA championship in 1950 sailing a B Sneakbox for Bay Head.

Later in 2000, Ghost would win the Worlds, but she did not repeat her winning ways in the years to come. To be sure, Ghost continued to sail and to win the occasional race, but Bill was more concerned about unfinished academic projects, and new boats with excellent skippers were joining the class. Already in 2001, the new Spy with Gary Stewart at the helm and Raven with Pete Stagaard steering appeared on the starting line. Others would follow. The boats were upgraded and well sailed.

Fig. 142

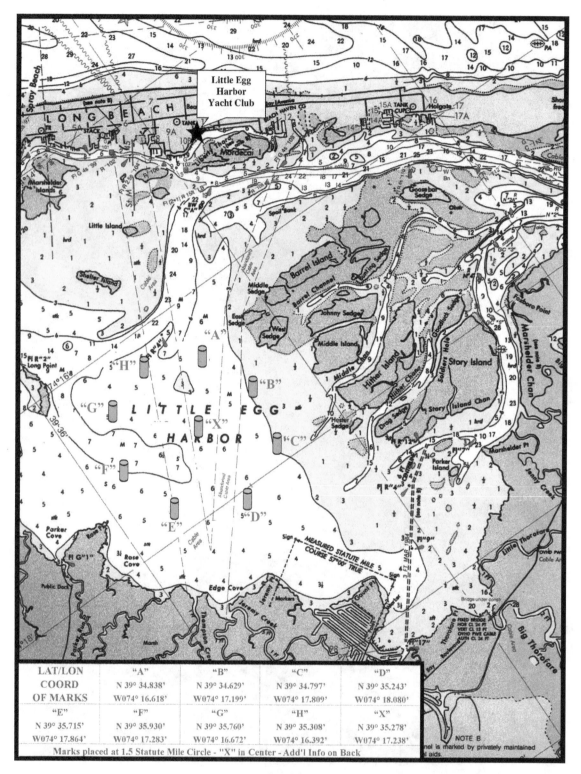

LAT/LON COORD OF MARKS	"A"	"B"	"C"	"D"
	N 39° 34.838'	N 39° 34.629'	N 39° 34.797'	N 39° 35.243'
	W074° 16.618'	W074° 17.199'	W074° 17.809'	W074° 18.080'
	"E"	"F"	"G"	"H"	"X"
	N 39° 35.715'	N 39° 35.930'	N 39° 35.760'	N 39° 35.308'	N 39° 35.278'
	W074° 17.864'	W074° 17.283'	W074° 16.672'	W074° 16.392'	W074° 17.238'

Marks placed at 1.5 Statute Mile Circle - "X" in Center - Add'l Info on Back

Fig. 143

VII
DOWN BAY TO LITTLE EGG

1. An Outstanding Race Course

"Little Egg" is short for "Little Egg Harbor," and "LEHYC" is short for the "Little Egg Harbor Yacht Club." The Club is located in Beach Haven on the southern end of Long Beach Island; it looks out on a body of water that is a continuation of Barnegat Bay, being some forty miles south of Bay Head and some thirty miles south of Seaside Park. It provides an outstanding race course, which is longer and wider than the upper and lower courses of the BBYRA. In addition, during summer months the Little Egg course is marked by excellent winds. Being separated from the ocean by a narrow strip of land, the sea breeze comes in as the strip and the mainland to the west heat up. That is also true to the north where the BBYRA races are held, but at Little Egg the wind is apt to fill in earlier and stronger before it works its way north.

The map reproduced here (fig. 143) shows the position of the LEHYC located on the western shore of Long Beach Island and to the East of Mordecai Island, which over the years has provided the club house and its docks with a measure of protection from storms coming out of the west. The cylinders pictured on the map mark the racing area. The cylinders sit on tall poles, which make them visible at a considerable distance. Together they constitute a fixed racecourse, in which cylinders "A" to "H" form a circle. The distance between opposite cylinders, i.e., the diameter of the circle, is 1.5 statute miles. Cylinder "X" is in the center of the circle and is used to create shorter legs. For many years this fixed course was a feature of the Down Bay Invitational Regatta, hosted by the LEHYC annually in August. In recent years moveable marks have been introduced, for now there are six or more fleets racing at the same time and the boats are unequal in speed. That produced crowding and occasionally harsh words as a fast boat attempted to push in front of slow boats at a turning mark. Moveable marks made it easy to create separate courses for different classes and thereby mitigated the problem of crowding.

Since 1928 the LEHYC has hosted the Barclay Cup, which is competed for by teams of junior sailors. The BBYRA clubs are invited, and over the years many youngsters have made the trip south to sail for the cup. Initially the trip was made by boat, towing fifteen foot Sneakboxes, which at Little Egg are known as "Perrines." When Comets replaced Sneakboxes and Optis replaced Comets, the trip was made by car, which shortened travel time by four hours, if the trip began in Bay Head. Ghost's owner-skipper, Bill Fortenbaugh, first made the tow in 1948, when he was ballast on a Sneakbox. Subsequently he skippered and his name can be found on the Barclay Cup. That began a quasi-romance with Little Egg, which has endured over many years, partly because some of Bill's Haverford School buddies still summer in Beach Haven—it has not entirely lost its Philadelphia roots—and partly because he has sailed frequently in the Down Bay Invitational. At first he sailed in Lightnings, later in M Scows, then in E Scows and finally in A Cats.

Since the Down Bay Invitational is regarded by many Barnegat Bay Sailors as the high point of the summer season, it is not surprising that the A Cats quickly became part of the regatta. The idea was initially advanced by Walter Smedley, who in 1994 sent a letter of congratulations to celebrate the launching of Ghost. The letter contained four lines of verse, which are recorded above (ch. V.2), followed by a suggestion:

With the advent of a new Flagship, how about a new venue?
Have Ghost lead the parade of the stately A Cats down to Little Egg
to be the highlight of our Invitational Regatta. We don't provide the
excitement of a search and find blind man's bluff, but we can give
you a good test of speed over uncongested waters.
And the party is fully up to the standards of an A Cat.

The suggestion could not have been better put. It flatters not only Ghost—"lead the parade"—but also the Class—"the stately A Cats"—and concludes with two persuasive truths: the Little Egg race course provides a fair test of boat speed, and the Saturday night party is a humdinger. The very next year, 1995, the A Cat fleet began sailing in the Invitational Regatta. Many of the A Cat crews were invited to overnight locally with club members—an admirable tradition at LEHYC—and all were treated both to good racing and to good rum, namely Mount Gay. Moreover, for many the most memorable moment occurred early on Saturday at the skippers' meeting. Walter would welcome the sailors, offer sage advice and close his remarks with a booming pronouncement, "It's a beautiful day in Beach Haven!"

2. The Rheingold Mug

When it was certain that A Cats would be racing at Little Egg in August 1995, the Ghost crew acted in character: it was decided to donate a trophy that would be awarded annually to the winning A Cat. And since worthy donors prefer anonymity, it was decided to give the cup a name that was appropriate to Ghost but made no direct reference to the boat or her crew. That caused some head scratching, until a crew member spoke against donating an elegant silver cup. He suggested an antique pewter mug: one that lacked a shiny surface, and was large enough to hold two pints of beer within and the names of winners on the outer surface. At a local antique store in Point Pleasant near Bay Head, the perfect mug was found. Agreeing on a name was now easy: The Rheingold Mug. There would be no reference to the donor, only to a popular beer. Younger sailors might have their thoughts drawn to Miss Rheingold, the beauty queen of the forties and fifties, while older sailors would be reminded that at the end of a race there would be waiting an "extra dry treat." And tradition determined that only the year and the name of the winning boat would be inscribed on the mug. Neither owner nor skipper would be recorded.

Fig. 144

Fig. 144 is a photo of the Rheingold mug. As stated, it is made of pewter, which is an alloy whose main ingredient is tin. The surface is matte or dull, appropriate for a drinking vessel at a local pub, and by no means inappropriate as a drinking vessel for A Cat sailors. Toward the top of the mug one reads the numeral "1" followed by the letter "l" in script. That means one liter (litre, English spelling), which is slightly more than one US liquid quart. The size is perfect: there are two pints in a quart, and Rheingold was available in quart bottles (see ch. V.3 on the quart bottle used in the baptism of Ghost). The first line of the inscription reads "THE RHEINGOLD MUG." Below that comes "A CAT FLEET" and below that "GHOST 1995," which was the first year of competition for the cup. Tradition determined that only the year and the name of the winning boat would be inscribed on the mug. The names of owners and/or skippers are not recorded. In the A Cat fleet, it's the boat that takes center stage.

The first year of competition saw Ghost win the Rheingold Mug, but she did not win again until the fourth year. In the intervening two years the winner was Mary Ann. That confirmed Walter's claim that the Little Egg race course would provide a good test of speed. Mary Ann had always exhibited speed upwind, and at Little Egg, when the wind increased and the bay began to kick up, she showed herself to be especially fast. Mary Ann was able to cut through a rolling, head-on sea, while Ghost had difficulty doing so. The likely explanation is that Mary Ann was built according to the Mower design and had a sloped bow, while Ghost was built according to a Sweisguth design with a noticeably blunter bow. Other factors were undoubtedly in play such as the length of the centerboard, the depth of the deadwood and the shape of the rudder. But there is more. Happily for Ghost, Mary Ann's speed upwind, albeit impressive, could be matched by the downwind speed, which Ghost had exhibited throughout her first season and continued to exhibit during the second. Again a difference in design seems to have been important. Ghost's full bow may have kept the boat from plowing in a following sea, and a slightly fuller transom may have kept the boat level fore and aft. Whatever the correct explanation, Ghost's downwind speed provided compensation: what she lost upwind she might reclaim downwind. Both boats needed to respond to these differences, albeit in different ways. Upwind Mary Ann needed to break free and put her speed to use. Downwind Ghost needed to keep Mary Ann in her wind shadow, overtake and pass Mary Ann before rounding the leeward mark. That called for well planned jockeying, which both Ghost and Mary Ann embraced. Fair enough, but at Little Egg in the 1990s the standard course was windward-leeward with the first leg to windward and the last leg to windward. That meant one more upwind leg, i.e., that to the finish line. On two occasions, 1996 and 1997, that decided the regatta, but it would be a mistake to overemphasize the advantages of either Mary Ann or Ghost. Chris Chadwick, the skipper of Mary Ann, was a skilled, experienced helmsman, who had put together a good crew. Much the same can be said of the Ghost crew. Moreover and more importantly, racing at Little Egg encouraged good sailing and good sportsmanship, which at night was transformed into a party, which was "fully up to the standards of an A Cat." Walter had it right.

In fig. 145, the crew of Ghost is shown in 1996 testing the waters at Little Egg prior to the first race of the Invitational Regatta. On the weather side of the boat from the rear are Ed, who is trimming the sail, and John and Rich; in front of them are John Coyle of Little Egg, and Jim Cadranell of Bay Head. The latter had become a regular member of Ghost's crew earlier in the year. Within the cockpit we see Bill wearing his familiar red life preserver and white tie-on hat; also Pat leaning over

Fig. 145

while attending to lines. High on the middle of the cabin top is Bev. The crew totals eight; John Coyle had come aboard in anticipation of heavy wind. Nineteen years later, he would be instrumental in bringing Ghost to the Maritime Museum in Beach Haven (ch. IX.1).

Ghost would win the Rheingold Mug three more times in 2002, 2006 and 2010. All three were sweet, for Ghost had slipped back into the pack: no longer the boat to beat but still capable of a decent regatta. That was especially true in 2006, when Ghost had three good races and was leading going into the last race, which she won. The other two wins, those of 2002 and 2010, were not only sweet but also especially memorable, for the outcome was in doubt until the last leg of the last race.

In 2002, Witch was dominant. She was new to the fleet and was showing her stuff. The boat was clearly fast and three weeks later would win the BBYRA championship. Moreover, the skipper was Russell Lucas, who had crewed on Ghost and at the time was widely regarded as the best of the Bay Head sailors. On Saturday Ghost had won a race and done well in a second, so that on Sunday Ghost and Witch were tied.

Whichever boat beat the other would win the regatta. At the start and for most of the race, the morning wind was light to moderate from the southeast. Ghost managed to hang close to Witch upwind and close the gap downwind. At the end of the second and next to last upwind leg, Ghost was some three boat lengths behind Witch. Benefiting from a series of puffs and keeping a distinct heel to weather in order to relieve the helm, Ghost slid past Witch downwind and opened a lead of two or three boat lengths before reaching the leeward mark. The question was whether Ghost would try to cover Witch or tack off on its own. Being a tad slower upwind, covering might fail, so that Ghost tacked off heading south. One might say that Ghost was rolling dice and hoping against hope, but the wind was building and this was Little Egg. It was not unreasonable to think that the wind might clock south and possibly a tad southwest, so that by going south initially Ghost would be able to tack on to a lift and approach the finish on a favorable angle. Apparently Witch was confident and let Ghost go, expecting to sail higher and a faster and to beat Ghost to the finish line. But that was not to be. The wind did clock into the south-southwest, and when the two boats crossed with the finish line in view, Ghost was still ahead and won the race. Hence, the regatta as well. Russell may have been kicking himself for not going south sooner, but he was gracious in congratulating Ghost, both at the finish line and back at dock.

Fig. 146 records a moment during the 2002 regatta at Little Egg. Most likely it is the first race on Saturday morning. What we see is Ghost leading the way. She had rounded the weather mark in front of Wasp and Witch and maintained her lead while reaching to the offset mark, where she would turn and run to the leeward mark. There she would round up and tack to the finish line, holding off both Wasp and Witch. Shown toward the front of Ghost's cabin is Betsy Hawkings. Along side her is Jennifer Miller. Wearing dark glasses is Ellyn Shannon. The person wearing red shorts cannot be identified. Next in blue shorts is Rich Miller, Ghost's big man and father of Jennifer. John Dickson in the rear is trimming the sail. The skipper is seated on a bench toward the rear of the cockpit and therefore cannot be seen.

In 2010 the regatta would again come down to the last race. The wind was moderate and Ghost needed to win. Throughout four legs, two upwind and two downwind, Ghost was in the hunt, never in front and never far behind. On the last weather leg to the finish line, the wind began building, puffing to fifteen plus knots, but the sea had not yet begun to kick up. Accordingly, Ghost would be beating to windward in relatively flat water. Bill instinctively began to take advantage of puffs by heading up ever so slightly, while maintaining a decent speed, and turning back when the wind slackened and before speed had been lost. That manner of steering is called feathering and is quite effective as long the skipper avoids sudden, jerky movements on the tiller. Bill had learned to feather as a youth while racing on the Metedeconk River, which rarely produced waves. In the afternoons the sea breeze would blow in

Fig. 146

Fig. 147

from the south but given the easterly direction of the river, rough water rarely occurred. Now on the Little Egg course, Bill found himself returning to a technique he
had learned many years before. It worked and Ghost, which was on port, crossed Spy
on starboard by inches. That was a gamble and it paid off. Ghost continued on port
while working to windward in puffs. Ghost soon crossed in front of Torch and Vapor,
immediately tacked onto starboard and went on to win the race and the regatta for
the last time. In fig. 147, we see Ghost ahead of Torch and Vapor and soon to cross
the finish line. Ghost's crew is riding the rail with legs overboard and Bill is taking
advantage of puffs, inching the boat to weather and then turning back as soon as the
wind began to moderate. Indeed, the photo shows Ghost pointing a degree or two
higher than Torch and markedly higher than Vapor.

For five more years Ghost would make the long tow from Bay Head to Little Egg in order to race for the Rheingold Mug. Ghost had some encouraging moments that recalled earlier successes and rekindled the desire to sail on the open waters off Beach Haven. Moreover, often impish, the crew of Ghost delighted in hoisting one of the larger Rheingold flags—Ghost had four—on the flagpole of the LEHYC. Typically the caper occurred on Saturday night, when the sailors were mellow on Mount Gay rum and absorbed in eating all the buffet had to offer. The flagpole was positioned to the side of the dining area, so that the crew of Ghost could do its work unnoticed. The Rheingold flag was hoisted well up the pole to a position above that of the commodore's flag. There it was fastened securely and there it would remain throughout the night. On Sunday morning the flag was still in place for all the sailors to behold. Happily the officers of the LEHYC had and still have a good sense of humor.

Despite such youthful behavior, the crew was getting up in years. Bill was seventy-nine, and with a single exception, the other members of the crew were over fifty, with some over sixty. Hence, in 2015 it was decided that Ghost should stay at Little Egg, where she would find a new home at the New Jersey Maritime Museum. Sensible, but also sad. For not only would Ghost fail to return to Bay Head on Sunday after the regatta, but also the crew would not be together on Ghost during the remainder of the season, not to mention summers to come. Nevertheless, team Ghost did its best to keep spirits high, to sail well and to party hard. Walter's characterization of the Saturday night Mount Gay bash still held true: it was "fully up to the standards of an A Cat" (ch. VII.1).

As a result, Sunday morning was a tad slow for the crew of Ghost, but the wind was light, so that the sail to the starting line was uneventful and even pleasant. In fig. 148 (next page), Ghost has just left the main dock of the LEHYC. The wind is light from the south. In front and to the right of Ghost is an E Scow, which also will sail to the starting line. Aboard Ghost we see Mark Kotzas sitting on the cabin top. Greg Matzat is steering and Bill is wearing his white hat. Mike Spark's head is visible behind Bill, and Dave Hoder is near the transom on the starboard side. The white shirt within the cabin is Robert Wahlers and the person in the dark shirt on the starboard side is Dylan Froriep, Greg's crew on his E Scow. Bill's bent-over head might suggest sadness—his last time on the starting line at Little Egg—but that is unlikely. More probably it is a residual effect of the Saturday night party, or is he looking at a sweet bun that has fallen on the floorboards?

Fig. 148

Fig. 149

In fig. 149, we see Ghost perhaps fifteen or twenty minutes later still sailing to the starting line. The time lag is not surprising given that the breeze is light and that at Little Egg an A Cat cannot sail a direct line from the harbor to the course. She must first twist and turn in a westerly direction thereby staying in the channel. Only after reaching deeper water can an A Cat head in a more northerly direction. That is what Ghost is doing having jibed from port to starboard tack.

Ghost finished the Sunday race somewhere in the middle and upon returning to dock was met by the wives of the crew. There was a call for last photos: first the crew face on (see ch. IV.3 fig. 94) and then with backs turned to indicate closure (fig. 150). The latter photo shows that Ghost's sail has been furled and the green sail cover put in place. Nevertheless the photo is not perfect—Greg Matzat had worn a non-conforming T-shirt—but his smile tells the viewer that Ghost's crew had not lost its sense of humor. Moreover and more important, when the crew departs, Casper the Ghost will remain behind, ready to spook the competitors as he has done for the last twenty-two years.

Fig. 150

VIII
THE CREW

1. Various Tasks Distributed among the Crew

First the word "crew." In regard to sailboats, it can be used with special reference to the shop and yard crew, i.e., the persons who build and maintain boats at a particular yard such as David Beaton & Sons. But that is not the primary use of "crew." Most often it refers to the sailors who are aboard a boat and actively engaged in making the boat sail. That includes not only the skipper but also the persons who work together with the skipper. Indeed, "crew" can be used narrowly of the latter: those persons who may not steer but are essential to sailing boats that require cooperation between two or more persons. This chapter will begin with brief remarks concerning the skipper, but the primary focus will be on the persons who join with the skipper in making a sailboat move through the water. We might call them the *sine quibus non*, those persons without whom the skipper cannot sail a boat, let alone win a race.

Throughout the sailing world, skippers exhibit a variety of attributes. The A Cat class is no exception: some skippers are muscular and others are lean; some are tall and some are short; some are still in college, while others have long been part of the work force. On days when the wind is light to moderate, the strength that comes with muscle is largely unimportant, but as the wind picks up, pressure on the helm begins to challenge the skipper. Upwind all but the strongest skippers will steer with two hands and with their feet placed firmly against braces on the cockpit floor. And on a downwind leg when a jibe is called for, the skipper is well advised to slow the turn of the boat at the very moment that the boom crosses from one side to the other. And that involves strength as well as timing (ch. VI.1 end).

Height is also a factor, for the skipper finds his place toward the rear of an A Cat, most often seated on the windward bench. When he steers upwind in a blow such that the boat is constantly heeling, the average skipper will have difficulty looking over the windward rail and seeing competitors who may be in front on the same tack. To be sure, there is the exceptional skipper who is quite tall or long in torso and neck. He finds it easier to look over the windward rail, but even he will have his view limited when heavy wind keeps the boat sailing on her side.

In addition, looking out to leeward and ahead can be all but impossible. For when the boat is heeled, the boom is lower, so that it blocks out competitors to

Fig. 151

leeward, who may be approaching on the opposite tack. In close competition that can be dangerous: it opens the door to a port-starboard infraction. Accordingly, the A Cat skipper must rely on others and in particular on the person trimming the sail. He is seated behind the skipper and normally on the windward deck, from which he can see around the rear of the sail as well as out to windward. That means he can see which of the competitors are doing better and which worse. Moreover, he can anticipate close crossings and advise the skipper whether to cross, tack under or pass behind a competitor approaching on starboard. In this regard, Ghost was fortunate to have Ed Vienckowski trimming sail. His calls contributed mightily to Ghost's early dominance in BBYRA competition.

The age of A Cat skippers varies considerably, but there are limits. Even though age brings experience, which every skipper needs, age eventually erodes strength. Four jibes over a ten-mile course in a strong breeze can be too much for an aging body. In this regard, youth has its attractions, but ruling out exceptional cases, a young person needs seasoning. In particular, he needs to learn his limitations and not try to do everything himself. That may seem obvious, but a skipper who has grown up racing a single-handed boat like a Laser might become impatient when the centerboard is slow to be lowered or raised. He is apt to reach for the centerboard line and lose concentration on the race course around him. Moreover, on downwind legs, a skipper should consider turning over the tiller to an experienced crew member like Ed's wife, Bev. Instead of riding the boom (ch. VI.2 fig. 149), she is pleased to have a turn steering (fig. 151), while the skipper benefits from a pause.

As indicated, a talented trimmer is important, but he too needs assistance from other members of the crew. That is especially true in heavy wind, when trimming the sail requires considerable strength, so that two strong men are better than one. At the start of a race when the skipper decides it is time to trim the sail and to bring the boat quickly up to full speed, two trimmers are called for. And when jibing or simply rounding a leeward mark without jibing, speed in trimming is important. Again two are better than one. And their work is efficient because the mainsheet on an A Cat is double ended. Each trimmer has his own end and pulls without disturbing the other. During the early years, John Dickson was the second trimmer and was always ready to fill in for Ed, should he need a breather. That brings the number of persons in the cockpit to three: helmsman plus two on the mainsheet. In fig. 152, we see John trimming the sail along with Robert Wahlers. That dates the photo to Ghost's middle years, c. 2004.

Fig. 152

Fig. 153

There are other tasks as well that require strength and expertise. One is making and breaking the port and starboard backstays. An exceptionally nimble person might be able to cross over the centerboard well with such quickness that he could both make and break the backstays by himself. But that is difficult and all but impossible in heavy air, so that two members of the crew are needed to deal with the backstays. In the beginning, they were Pat Jurczak and Rich Miller. That brings the number of people in the cockpit to five. And when adjusting the centerboard up or down before rounding a mark and changing the tension on the luff and the foot of the sail are added to the mix, everyone in the cockpit has more than enough to do.

In fig. 153, Ghost is in the process of rounding a mark of the course (a large yellow buoy) on the starboard side of the boat. Dan Crabbe is steering, while the sail is being trimmed by Greg Matzat, who is sitting on the weather deck, and by Marty Masterson, who is on his feet to leeward. (Marty crewed for Greg on the latter's E Scow). The windward backstay is tight and the centerboard is down. Judging from the boat, which is visible behind Ghost, Dan is likely to have approached the buoy on starboard tack, so that it was not necessary to jibe or come about in order to round the mark. The centerboard will have been lowered prior to the rounding in preparation for tacking upwind. Clearly the crew within the cockpit has been busy and successful in accomplishing its appointed tasks. That said, it is well to acknowledge that there are occasions when the cockpit crew—individually or as whole—can and do lose control. See the Appendix to section 1 of this chapter.

There remains the foredeck crew. An A Cat regularly sails both upwind and on a reach with one person, or more commonly with two people, on the rail in front of the side stays. And when the wind is strong, a third might be added, depending on size. In a strong wind with a heavy sea, riding the rail up front is certainly a wet job and sometimes unpleasant, but the added weight is important not only to minimize sideward heeling but also to balance the boat fore and aft. It is tempting to diminish the persons who ride the rail upwind and across the wind as "rail meat," persons who are valued for the size of their bodies and little else. But that is quite unfair. Going upwind involves tacking and that calls for changing sides quickly: using hand rails on the top of the cabin and grabbing the mast or forestay when moving from side to side. A slow response is likely to impede the tack and a clumsy response can result in one or more persons overboard. Moreover, some quite good sailors are known to have ridden the rail on Ghost. One thinks of Rod Edwards, Jim Cadranell and John Harkrader.

In fig. 154, we see Ghost preparing to come about. Up front on the windward side of boat are two members of the foredeck crew: the foremost person is unidenti-

Fig. 154

Fig. 155

fied; in the second position partially hidden is Mark Kotzas. Anticipating the tack, the foremost person has already grabbed the handrail and begun to pull herself up. Mark has also begun to elevate himself. They will work their way around the mast holding on to the side stays and the forestay. Since the sea is calm, moving in this manner should not be difficult.

In fig. 155, the same crew is approaching a mark. And again we see the foremost member of the crew beginning to arise in anticipation of changing course, perhaps by jibing around the mark. It appears that Ghost has overshot the weather mark and therefore has headed off in order to gain speed. That should help Ghost stay in front of the boat that is in close pursuit. It might seem that Robert Wahlers, who is squatting on the leeward side, has his foot dragging in the water. But most likely his foot is firmly planted on the leeward rail; it is spray that creates a false impression.

Whether jibing or tacking the members of the foredeck crew must maintain their balance when rounding the mast. Failure to do so could result in "man overboard." Ghost rarely experienced "man-overboard," but it did happen with differing results. On one occasion during the Callahan Regatta (held annually by the Bay Head Yacht Club on the last Friday in July), it required turning back, thereby going from first to last and losing the regatta. On another occasion, during the Little Egg Invitational (ch. 7.1), the big man, Rich Miller, responded with extraordinary alertness. He

Fig. 156

reached over the side and pulled Ellyn Shannon out of the water before Ghost sailed past her. Hurrah for Rich and hurrah for Ellyn. Her error would not be repeated. In fact, she became one of Ghost's most dependable foredeck crew. See fig. 156: Ellyn is riding the foredeck with Deezi Lindenmayer. They are at ease, while the skipper concentrates. Such a mixture—untroubled attention—makes a boat fast.

Riding the boom is an A Cat specialty that occurs on downwind legs. One member of the foredeck crew rides, i.e., sits on the boom, while others retreat to the cockpit and play a role in controlling the heel of the boat. Keeping one person forward sitting on the boom is a consequence of the large size of the sail. In medium to heavy wind, the sail is apt to belly out and lift the boom thereby diminishing sail area and the forward thrust of the wind. And in light air, waves from other boats, especially motorboats, are apt to rock the boat and cause the boom to jerk up and down, thereby causing the sail to lose wind. But there is also reason not to place a person on the boom. In order to be effective in holding the boom down, that person must be some distance out to leeward on the boom and away from the centerline of the boat. That increases the tendency of the boat to heel to leeward, which promotes a weather helm. To compensate, the skipper must be continually working the tiller to keep the boat moving forward. When that happens, the rudder acts as a brake, which is slow. Hence, when the air is moderate and the water relatively flat, it is often advantageous not to place a person on the boom, but rather to add that person's weight to the weather side. That will make it possible to heel the boat to weather, thereby reducing the helm and increasing speed. But in a heavy wind with a following sea, the primary concern is steadying the boat as it pushes ahead. Indeed, heeling the boat to weather in order to eliminate helm and increase speed is no longer a consideration, for the boat will have reached hull speed: she is too heavy to lift out of the water and plane along the surface.

In the early years, Rod Edwards and Bev Vienckowski were regular members of the foredeck crew, and when a third was needed, Rich Miller's daughter Jennifer was a person of choice. Later the persons riding up front would change. Already at the end of the second year, Rod retired and was replaced by Jim Cadranell (ch. VI.2). Soon Ellyn Shannon and later Mark Kotzas would be up front. There would also be short-term replacements, especially at Little Egg. Commitments back home kept some crew members away, so that friends from Bay Head like Betsy Hawkings (ch. VII.2 fig. 146) would make the trip south, and members of the LEHYC were pleased to come aboard: e.g., John Coyle (ch. VII.2 fig. 145).

The above-mentioned tasks are perhaps the most important, but there are other tasks as well. For example, when the starting line is long, so that the skipper will have difficulty judging when he is on the line but not over the line, a crew member—one with a good eye and a reliable sense of timing—may stand on the deck next to the starboard side stay, from where he can advise the skipper how close he is to the line and how fast he is approaching it. The Little Egg Invitational is a good example. There the E Scows start before the A Cats. Their numbers are large, say thirty boats, which demands a line much longer than that required for starting ten A Cats. Since the Regatta Committee is concerned with running races in a timely manner, it does not pause in the middle of the starting sequence to reset the line. Accordingly, the A Cats are confronted by an unnecessarily long line, which challenges the judgment of the skipper. When the wind is moderate so that falling off the boat is not a serious possibility, a wise skipper may well call upon a crew member who is sure footed to assist him, so that at the gun he is neither late nor early. Rather he has the boat trimmed down and moving fast, only a foot or two behind the line.

Quite different is the crew's role in reefing (shortening) the sail in anticipation of heavy wind. That requires several people, who know how to shorten the sail along the mast and the boom, and how to tie reefing lines around the boom in such a way that the tie is not only secure but also easily removed, should the wind moderate. When reefing is accomplished while still at dock or tied up to a towboat, the procedure is not especially challenging, but when it is done in the middle of a race, it is best started on a downwind leg and finished while going to windward, when the boom is over the boat so that reefing lines can be attached to the boom (assuming they are needed). Removing a reef is far simpler, although removing ties around the boom can only be done when the boom is over the boat or at least within arm's reach, which means during an upwind leg.

Still a different task is one for everybody but the skipper. It is called for when an A Cat runs aground in such shallow water that the deadwood is dragging. That is most likely to happen in unfamiliar water, but it can happen when the crew, skipper included, is having too much fun or simply inattentive. A different culprit may be the regatta committee, if it is using fixed buoys (not movable marks) and chooses to send the A Cat fleet from one buoy to another across shallow water. That is known to have happened at Seaside Park, when the assigned course kept the A Cats close to the eastern shore on the way north toward the Mathis Bridge. There the water is quite shallow, and on a day when the Bay is unusually low, the A Cats drag almost to a halt. The remedy is on one level humorous. The rear of the deadwood and the trailing rudder must be lifted up, and that can only be accomplished by sending everybody but the skipper forward, crowding around the mast and hanging on to stays. That has always worked for Ghost, but it is no fun for the skipper or whoever pays the bills. Quite apart from disturbing the race, the deadwood is getting a serious scraping and the rudder could be damaged as it once was off Shore Acres (ch. II.6.2).

Appendix to ch. VIII.1
Out of Control

Above the emphasis has been on the duties of the crew with little attention given to failure. To be sure brief notice was taken of clumsiness and losing a crew member overboard, but more might have been said. Here in an appendix that omission will

Fig. 157

be made good by calling attention to a truly frantic moment when various errors resulted in Ghost tipping over.

In fig. 157, Ghost is clearly out of control; the crew is struggling to avoid tipping over. But what went wrong is uncertain. Dan Crabbe says that he was skippering Ghost in a three race series for the Wanamaker Cup. The location is the mouth of Toms River with the wind blowing southeast and freshening just prior to the starting gun of the second race. Being early for the start and being at the leeward end of the line on starboard tack, Dan decided to bail out by jibing around the leeward pin onto port tack and passing behind the fleet, which was on starboard tack. That way Ghost might be able to pick up speed, while sailing free of other boats, and cross the starting line at the windward end. The idea was not foolish, but the execution was less than perfect. Dan had forgotten his training as an engineer. He was familiar with centrifugal force and should have remembered Newton's law of motion: a body in motion tends to stay in motion unless acted upon by an outside force. So it was with Ghost. When Dan slammed the tiller down, hoping to round up quickly, the tip of the mast arched across the sky and then headed straight for the water, taking Ghost and her crew into the water. (See above ch.VI.1, the penultimate paragraph on tripping over the centerboard.) Perhaps the crew member assigned to centerboard duty was also at fault. He may have been inattentive and failed to raise the board. Or was he given insufficient warning of Dan's intended maneuver? Either way the crew experienced Ghost rolling onto its side before sinking into the water.

A different account is offered by Dave Hoder, who says Bill was the skipper—an assertion that Bill denies. The photo offers neither confirmation nor refutation. The skipper seems to have slipped or fallen onto the floor of the cockpit and so out of sight. Be that as it may, Dave says that during the jibe from starboard to port tack, the boom came across the boat so fast that the starboard backstay could not be loosened quickly enough to allow the boom to run its normal course. The sail wanted to keep going, which it did, taking the whole boat over with it. Perhaps the person assigned to loosening the weather backstay was a contributor to the disaster. His mind was elsewhere, so that he was too late to free the backstay. In any case, John Dickson, who is seen struggling with the sheet, was first in the water with the others following in quick order. That would include the person who is clinging to the mast. The photo shows only an arm and a hand, but it is easy to imagine a member of the foredeck crew being surprised and even frightened by the suddenness of the jibe.

Fig. 158

2. A Special Appreciation

In concluding this chapter on the crew, it seems appropriate to single out one member of team Ghost for special mention. That person is John Dickson, who was part of the Ghost team from beginning to end, i.e., the twenty-two seasons beginning with the launching of Ghost in summer 1994 and running through summer 2015. Only Bill can claim an equal number of years, but that is nothing special, for he was the owner and in the early years the regular skipper of Ghost. The continued association of John and Bill goes back to E Scow sailing, and as mentioned above, it was John who first suggested the name "Ghost" (ch. I.2). In 1996 John began using his motorboat to tow Ghost not only to the Saturday BBYRA races but also to special trophy races. To the latter category belongs the Little Egg Invitational Regatta, in which A Cats compete for the Rheingold Mug (ch. VII.2). The tow to Little Egg was long and not inexpensive. All who sailed on Ghost are appreciative of what John contributed.

In the person of John, generosity and loyalty were mixed with a tenacious courage that often went unnoticed. That is, of course, how John wanted it, but his dealing with cancer for over twenty-two years was remarkable. When John was racing on Bill's E Scow in the early 1990s, he developed leukemia and underwent a bone marrow transplant at the Memorial Sloan Kettering Cancer Center in New York City. The treatment was effective and John was able to join Bill in putting together team Ghost. But the treatment also weakened his back, so that he had difficulty standing up straight. Eventually he had struts placed in his upper body, which produced some improvement, but not enough to keep racing on Ghost. Nevertheless, John did not walk away in self-pity. Instead, he continued to tow Ghost to regattas and to go for the occasional pleasure sail. In fig. 158 (preceding page), we see Ghost with nine persons board, enjoying an afternoon on the water. Bill is steering and John is trimming the sail, which he could still do even as his back began to worsen. He even tried racing a Sandpiper with Mark Kotzas. But cancer returned, and in the fall of 2015 John died. We might say that he departed with Ghost. For after the Little Egg Invitational, John and Bill motored back to Bay Head, leaving Ghost in Beach Haven. It was a sad trip, not least because the pleasure of watching Ghost glide through the water was missing. Now John is missing and the Ghost team has broken up.

In memory of John, this chapter ends with a wonderful photo of Ghost under tow (fig. 159). An afternoon of racing is over. Day is slowly giving way to night, and clouds are gathering. The sun is still able to light up the water on Ghost's port side. Her tall mast appears as a silhouette reaching upward in the sky. An impressive sight that many a crew member enjoyed thanks to John's loyalty over more than two decades.

Fig. 159

IX
A NEW HOME

At the conclusion of the 2015 Down Bay Invitational Regatta, Ghost's crew returned to points north, while Ghost herself stayed behind tied up to the main dock of the Little Egg Harbor Yacht Club. An anchor had been put out to ensure that Ghost would remain a safe distance off the dock. That was a last act of seamanship by Ghost's crew. The future lay with John Coyle, a member of the LEHYC, who together with his wife Gretchen saw in Ghost an opportunity to bring an A Cat to lower Barnegat Bay and to enhance the mission of the New Jersey Maritime Museum. Their vision was faultless and would have won applause from Walter Smedley, who some twenty-one years earlier wrote a prescient letter to celebrate the launching of Ghost. He urged the A Cat fleet to travel south and to participate in the Invitational Regatta. A year later the fleet did come and the folk at Little Egg were pleased with what they saw. Walter had it right, when he described the A Cats as "stately" and noted that the "uncongested" waters of the Little Egg race course would provide a fair test of speed (see ch.VII.1).

The New Jersey Maritime Museum is relatively young, being founded ten years ago, but its roots go back more than two decades, when Deborah Whitcraft began collecting information concerning shipwrecks along the Jersey coast. Her collection of files and physical memorabilia grew over the years and found a home in the Museum, when it opened its doors in 2007. That collection has continued to be updated and is today the primary attraction within the walls of the Museum. But outside the walls, the Museum was lacking. Despite being housed a stone's throw from the bay, the Museum had no boats afloat that might introduce people to traditional boating and do so under sail. That lack was noticed by John Coyle, who made it his mission to remedy the situation by bringing A Cats to the Museum. He knew that the boats had become expensive not only to build but also to maintain in racing condition. That meant a weak market, so that there were owners who were prepared to donate their boats to a registered non-profit museum. A fair appraisal meant a worthwhile tax deduction, which was attractive to several owners including Bill Fortenbaugh, the owner of Ghost. John did not hesitate to approach Bill and soon persuaded him to transfer ownership of Ghost to the Museum. Not long thereafter John persuaded the syndicate that owned Raven, Ghost's sister ship, to do the same.

Such transfers are, of course, two sided. Not only must the donor be willing to turn over a valuable boat, but the recipient Museum must be willing take on a new responsibility. Here tax law played a role. Originally the Executive Director of the Maritime Museum, Jim Vogel, thought that the Museum would keep Ghost for three years as required by law and then sell the boat. The money could be used for other purposes. But the Director and other officers of the Museum came to think otherwise. In October 2016, Jim wrote in a letter to Bill, "We (and I personally) have been captivated by the beauty of the boat and the tradition of the class. Our plan now is to keep the Ghost and to sail her for the long term." A wise decision that would apply to Raven as well.

There was no one event during the summer of 2016 that persuaded the directors of the Museum to embrace Ghost and Raven and to do so for years to come. Rather it was the many uses and worthwhile occasions that determined the director's decision. Perhaps most impressive is the contribution that Ghost and Raven made to junior sailing programs on Long Beach Island. Jim Vogel has put the number of children involved at 500 (*"Catting Around Barnegat Bay"* p. 39). That is surely no exaggeration, for an A Cat easily holds ten youngsters, and there are more than a few sailing centers on the Island: e.g. the yacht clubs at Spray Beach, Brandt Beach and Surf City as well as the LEHYC. John Coyle reports that the idea behind moving the A Cats "around the various local yacht clubs was to show young sailors that they can continue their sailing careers on classic boats that afford them the chance to refine their sailing skills absent many of the modern gadgets that adorn many of today's sailboats" (ibid.) That is correct, only it is equally important that kids discover that sailing is fun, whether or not they become skilled helmsmen or sought after mainsheet tenders.

Fig 160 speaks volumes. There are eleven kids aboard and all are expressing their delight as the wind begins to kick in. To be sure, eleven kids are too many for racing, but at the moment Ghost is not trying to win a race. Rather, she is introducing youngsters to the joy of sailing. And with so many aboard, not only is adult supervision mandatory but so also are life vests for the kids.

Fig. 160

Very special was bringing Ghost north to Bay Head in June for the Wounded Veterans' Sail. There was some racing, but caution was the rule, so that boats reefed when the wind was still modest. In fig. 161 Ghost is pictured under way. The Yacht Club has been left behind and soon Ghost will be in open water at the mouth of the Metedeconk River. There appear to be six people in the cockpit and one person well forward almost in front of the mast on the windward side. He seems to be dealing with the painter or bowline, making sure that it does not fall overboard, now that it is no longer being used to tie Ghost to the Club dock.

Having a crew member so far forward on the deck is not normally recommended: it weighs the bow down, so that it plows water and slows the boat. But on this occasion, having someone well forward counteracts the weight of the people aft, so that the bow is not unduly lifted out of the water. The modest bow wave off the starboard side tells us that the boat is for the moment adequately balanced fore and aft. Ideally some of the people in the cockpit should move forward and sit on the deck alongside the cabin, and the person forward should move aft and join them alongside the cabin. But most of the persons in the cockpit are wounded veterans, who are better off remaining in place. There they are enjoying the sail, which is the primary goal of the Wounded Veterans Sail. We might say that Ghost is "giving back" in her own way.

Participation by Ghost in the Callahan regatta in Bay Head on the last Friday in July and in the BBYRA race the following Saturday at Shore Acres provided excitement for an adult crew made up of sailors from both ends of Barnegat Bay. There are plans for greater involvement by both Ghost and Raven on northern waters next summer, 2017, but time will tell. The upbay sailors who have been coming to the Invitational Regatta for two decades will attest that the trip is long and often tiring, but also worthwhile.

Finally, there was involvement by Ghost in the Down Bay Invitational, where local sailing instructors formed the bulk of the crew. Exceptional were several seasoned sailors, Dave Hoder and Rich O'Such, who came aboard on Saturday as the wind picked up, and Jim Vogel, who replaced Rich on Sunday. Finishes were not great, but a third in the second race on Saturday was no mean feat for a largely novice crew.

Fig. 161

· This chapter ends the story of Ghost's journey From *Beaton's to Beach Haven*. A final photo shows Ghost and Raven happily at anchor in front of Mordicai Island, only a short distance west of the LEHYC. It is late in the day. Ghost is flying a flag, while Raven is at rest nearby (fig. 162).

The flag is new to Ghost. It exhibits a copy of the ghost (Casper look-alike) that is sewn on Ghost's green sail cover and visible in the photo. The flag replaces the Rheingold flags—four in total—that were flown by Ghost in its first life. Members of the original crew will be saddened, but truth be known the change makes sense, for Rheingold is no longer available. The brewery went belly up, so that each year fewer people recognize the name. Indeed today's youngsters are sure to draw a blank.

Fig. 162

INDEX OF SUBJECTS

The present "Index of Subjects" is focused on Ghost *qua* wooden boat of impressive size. It is intended to aid readers interested in the construction of a twenty-eight foot catboat and in that boat's successes and failures as a racing craft. Accordingly, the index is in large measure a guide to the parts and procedures involved in building Ghost, and to the adjustments and tactics that determined Ghost's finishes on the race course. In contrast, the index does not focus on individual persons. Exceptional are the proper names that are used commonly in reference to a business or location: e.g., Moorhouse Sails and Cattus Island.

Ablative paint] 87
Aground, runs] 78, 168-9
"Anchors Away"] 116
Anti-fouling paint] 86-7, 129, 135
Athwart timbers] 45-6

Baptism] 112-16
Barclay Cup] 149-50
Barnegat Bay Yacht Racing Association, BBYRA] 1-3, 104-5, 117-46, 149, 178
Base line] 24
Bat, A Cat] 1-8, 11, 18, 71, 108-09
Battens; batten pockets] 97
Battery] 70
Beam] cabin 66; deck 17, 35, 45-53, 57, 67
Beam] of an A Cat, see Width]
Beaton Sails] 97-100
Beaton's] see David Beaton and Sons
Bedlog] 27-9, 31-4, 45, 72
Bending jig] 60-2
Bending wood] 15-16, 38-9, 59-62
Benjamin River Marine] 6
Bilge stringers] 35, 45, 76
Blanket, downwind] 137
Boiler] 15, 61
Boom, spar] 92-6, 98, 119; sitting on, riding 139, 167
Bossett Sails] 96
Bow] 17-18, 67, 101, 113-15, 152
Bowline] 122
Box for steaming wood] 15-16, 36
Bozo the cat] 16, 85
Brace] to the ceiling 34, 39, 41; supporting the carling 46
Bucking Dolly] 59

Cabin] 15, 17, 59-71, 81-3
Callahan regatta] 166, 178
Camber, sail] 94
Canvas] 65
Capsize] see Tip over
Carling] 46-51
Casper the Ghost] 97, 100, 159
Caulking cotton] 42
Cedar] 16, 39-40, 52, 69
Ceiling, cabin] 70
Centerboard] 27-8, 72-4, 104, 164
Centerline] 19, 24-5, 34, 46-7
Ceremony] launching 106-16, awards 139-40
Chainplate] 30, 118
Challenge Cup] see Toms River
Christening] see Baptism
Clamp] 34
Coaming] 63-5
Cockpit] 17-18, 63, 71
Cod fish] 92-3
Compression strip] 61
Copper paint] 87
Core structure] 25-32
Corner patch, reinforcement] 94, 97-8
Cover, sail] 100, 159, 180
Cover, upwind] 137
Crew] 111, 161-170
Cunningham hole, sail] 94

Daggerboard] 73
David Beaton and Sons] 6, 13, 161
Deadwood] 28, 31-2, 74-9, 86, 135, 168-9
Deck] 17, 46-53, 57, 65, 84

Development class] 4-6, 89, 136

Doors] 69, 81-2, 120

Double ended sheet]163

Doubling pieces] 32

Downwind] 9, 75, 129, 152, 154, 167-8

Draft, sail] 75, 97

Drift rods] 72

Drip caps] 69

Duck Boat] 10, 73, 76, 87

Enemies] 5-6

Entryway] 69-70, 81-2, 104

Epoxy] 32, 52-3, 65, 71, 76-7, 84, 93

E Scow] 9-11, 74-5, 87, 97, 112, 134, 150, 157, 172

Evolution] see Development

Fairing] the ribs 38, with paste 85-6

Feathering] 154, 156

Fiberglass] 71, 73, 77

Filling, epoxy, putty] 53

Fir] 34-5

Flag, Rheingold] 56, 142-4, 146, 157; Ghost 180

Flat water] 154

Floor] 69-71, temporary 46

Floor frames] 28, 33-4, 36-7, 45

Foot braces] 121, 128, 161

Foot, sail] 97, 164

Forcem, A Cat] 1, 3, 6-7, 9, 18

Foredeck crew] 142, 164-8, 170

Framing] 32-8, 46, 51

Gaff, spar] 3-4, 8, 18, 89-92

Garboard plank] 27, 39, 43, 108

Gem, B Cat] 3

Ghost, A Cat] passim

Glass cloth] see Fiberglass

Glue] 32, 63, 76-7, 93-4

"God Bless America"] 112

Golden rivet] 58

Gold leaf] 86

"Great Ship Titanic"] 127

Green, dark] hull, topsides 60, 87-8, 100, 104, centerboard 104, sail cover 100, 159, 180

Green Island course] 134

G Sloop] 10, 87-8, 105, 121

Gudgeon] 57, 75-6, 86 -7

Handrail] 165

Hatch, sliding cover] 70-1, 92

Headledges] 27, 31, 45, 72

Heeling to weather] 154, 167

Helen, A Cat] 1, 18, 88, 109

Hinged, tiller] 76, 79

Hopper's Basin] 1, 7

Hull] 17-23

Hull speed] 10, 168

Independence Seaport Museum] 4, 6, 10, 109

Insignia] 11, 92, 97-8

Invitational Regatta] 136, 149-59, 166, 172, 175, 178

Jackstand] 41, 44, 113

Jibe] 10, 130-1, 161, 163, 170

Junior sailing program] 176

Keel] 26, 31-2, 34, 72-3, 92, 109

King-plank] 118

Kirk, builder] 1, 7

Knee, vertical hanging and horizontal lodging] 30, 32, 35, 49-53,

Laminate] 66, 76

Last Rivet Party] 54-9

Lateral resistance] 72-4

Launching] 101-16

Lead] 69, 72

Leech, sail] 75, 92, 94, 97

Length, overall and waterline] 8, 14

Lightning, A Cat] 24, 30

Little Egg Harbor Yacht Club, LEHYC] 112, 149-59, 175-6, 180

Locust, black/yellow] 79

Loft, sail] 97-8

Lofting, patterns] 9, 24, 33

Lostrom's shop] 6

Lotus, A Cat] 1, 6-7, 13, 18, 71, 109

Lower bay race course] 129, 130, 134, 136, 144

Luff, sail] 94. 97-8, 164

Mahogany] 15, 26, 28, 39, 47, 52, 59-61, 63, 67-9, 72, 76, 82, 83, 86

Map] see Race course

Marconi rig] 3- 7, 18, 89-94

Maritime Museum] see New Jersey Maritime Museum

Mary Ann, A Cat] 1-7, 18-19, 71, 89, 93, 109, 137-9, 152

Mast] 4, 17, 89-94, 108, 117-19, 126, 165-6
Masthead fly] 119
Mast hole] 49, 53
Mast partner] 53
Mast step] 29, 32, 93
Metedeconk River] 134, 154
Molds] 34, 39, 41, 45
Moorhouse Sails] 96
Mordicai Island] 149, 180
Mortise and tenon] 82, 94
Morton Johnson, builder] 1, 7, 9-10
Mower, naval architect] 1-9, 152
M Scow] 9, 87, 105, 112, 150
Mug] see Rheingold

New Jersey Maritime Museum] 153, 175-6
Nib scarf] 63

Oak] 26, 29, 33, 35, 50; white 15, 27, 35, 44; red 36
Offset table] 19, 23
Oil finish] 83-4
Oil furnace] 15
Old Overholt] 54-7, 107
Overboard, man] 165-6

Painter] see Bowline
Paste, wood-filler] 86
Patterns, lofting] 24, 33
Pegs, wooden] 43-4
Pennants] 104-5, 107, 140, 143
Perrine] 74
Philadelphia Maritime Museum] see Independence
Pivoting board] 73
Planking] 39-45
Pleasure sail] 171-2
Plumb line] 24-5, 47
Plywood] 17, 43, 52-3, 57, 65-7, 72, 76-8, 82
Primer, paint] 84-5

Rabbet] 30
Race course] BBYRA 123, 134; LEHYC 149
Rail meat] 165
Rake] mast 92-4; gaff 89
Raven, A Cat] 8, 11, 24, 26, 30, 146, 175-6, 180
Reef, sail] 94-7, 124, 129, 168
Rescue operation] 126
Rheingold] 54-7, 105-08, 110, 112, 140-6; mug 151-2,
    157, 172; umbrella 146

Rib] 15, 17, 35-8, 45, 53, 67
Ribband, temporary] 34-7, 39, 41
Riding the boom] see Boom
Rigging ladder] 103, 117-20
Rivet] 54-8, 86
Roof, cabin] 66-7
Rub rail] 39, 84
Rudder] 28, 74-9, 86, 135-6, 169
Rudderpost] 28, 75-6

Sail] 89-100
Sailfish] 73, 76
Scarfing] 35, 52, 63, 83
Scott II, B Cat] 2
Screening, cabin] 82
Seaside Park course] 134
Seaside Park Yacht Club] 139-40, 143, 146
Seats] 121, 128, 161-2
Sewell Cup] 2, 139-40, 143-4, 146
Sheer plank, strake] 35, 39
Sheer stringers] 35, 45
Shutter plank] 41
Sideslip] 72-4
Sitka spruce] 35, 93
Skeg] 28
Skipper] 142, 161-2
Slides, sail] 97-8
Sneakbox] 10, 60, 74, 87, 105, 112, 121, 146, 149
Sole] see Floor
Southerly shift, wind] 137, 154
Spars] 4, 89-96
Spectra] 6, 136
Splash rail] 60
Spreaders] 92, 94
Spy, A Cat] 1-7, 11, 13, 71, 88, 108-09, 146, 156
Spyder, A Cat] 11
Starting line] 129, 168, 170
Stays, fore, side and back] 17, 30, 89, 92, 118-20, 128, 136,
    163-5, 170
Steam box] 15-16, 36, 61
Stem] 26, 30, 44
Storage, winter] 135
Stove, wood-fired] 15, 38, 43
Strake] see Sheer plank
Straps, steel and bronze] 17, 49-51
Stringer, permanent 34-7
Stub-mast, stump] 94, 104-5, 117
Students' Waltz] 146

Sunfish] 55

Swedish rig] 3-5, 7-8, 18, 89-90

Sweisguth, naval architect] 1, hull plans 17-23, 49-51, 53,
   70, 72, 75, 78, 116; sail plans 71, 89-92

Tamwock, A Cat] 1-7, 17-18, 89-93, 109

Tenon] see Mortise and Tenon

Tiller] 79-80

Tip over] 10, 55, 124-5, 130, 169-70

Titanic] see "Great Ship Titanic"

Toe rail] 39, 84,118

Toilet] 18

Toms River Challenge Cup] 2-3

Torch] 156

Towline] 120, 122

Transom] 26, 31-2, 50, 86, 103, 109-10, 139

Travel lift on rails] 102-3, 113

Trimming, sail] 64-5, 142, 152, 162-4

Tripod, metal] see Jackstand

Truit, builder] 2

Trunk] see well

Upper bay race course] 124, 129, 134

Upwind] 18-19, 92, 97-8, 129, 130, 152, 154-6, 162, 168

Vapor, A Cat] 6, 88, 109, 136-9, 156

Varnish] 60, 70, 79, 83-5, 93, 135

Ventilation] 70-1, 79, 81, 84

Virginia, B Cat] 2

Wallowing] 74

Wanamaker] course 134, 144; trophy 130, 136, 169

Wasp, A Cat] 6, 8, 11, 13, 17-18, 24, 52, 71, 108-09, 139,
   154

Waterline] 6, 8, 17, 84, 116

Weather helm] 28, 74-5, 79, 94, 97

Well, centerboard] 27, 31, 34, 45, 57, 67, 72-4, 163

Width, A Cat] 8, 14, 18

Window, cabin] 70

Windward-leeward course] 152

Witch, A Cat] 11, 153-4

Woodshop] 13-16, 97, 101

Worlds] 131, 136, 146

Wounded Veterans' Sail] 178

Xynole] 17, 53, 62, 65, 71, 84